I PROMISE YOU

BARRETT BOYS EPILOGUE NOVELLA

JORDAN FORD

FLP

ISBN: 978-1-99-103465-6 (Paperback)
ISBN: 978-1-99-115136-0 (Kindle)

Forever Love Publishing Ltd
www.foreverlovepublishing.com

NOT ONE OF THEM

Jackson

I WALK OUT of the bathroom, adjusting my shirt before running my fingers through my hair, mussing the thick spikes so they sit the way I want them to. Who needs a comb, right?

The smell of fried bacon reaches me before I even hit the stairs, but I'm too distracted to really appreciate them this morning.

Prom.

Yep, my first one.

Advertising for the big event started popping up around school yesterday, and I know exactly who I'll be taking. We made a deal four years ago that we'd go together, and a promise is a promise.

I swallow, wondering how hard it's going to be. Things have changed since that day in the sunshine, but it's not like I can just pretend I've forgotten. It's Hailey. And if I'm honest, I actually want to go with her.

Because it's Hailey.

And everything about her is good.

Pushing up my sleeves, I jog down the stairs to breakfast. Arley is already at the table, looking cute as Deeks braids her hair while she munches on toast. He's become quite the expert with hair, and it always makes Kena's face go gooey. She gives him this smile which I can't decide is sweet or disgusting. Her eyes sometimes do this thing where she looks like she wants to haul him upstairs and jump his bones.

I'm sixteen. I really don't need to see that, especially just before eating my breakfast.

Jumping off the last step, I walk to the table and say good morning to Kena, kiss Arley on the cheek, and raise my eyebrows at Deeks.

He returns the favor, then concentrates on Arley's braids.

"You sleep okay last night?" Kena asks, delivering a fresh plate of toast to the table. "I heard you playing music until quite late."

I give her a closed-mouth smile. "I was playing it quietly. Just messing around on my guitar."

"Oh, I know. It's just a school night, that's all."

Plunking into my chair, I roll my eyes, and Kena immediately apologizes. "I know. I know. I'm not your mother. Sorry." Kissing the top of my head, she musses up my hair and disappears into the kitchen.

She's right. She's not my mother. I don't have one of those. What I have is this weird combination of an older sister who bosses me around and then multiple adults in their twenties who all act like my parents, then apologize when they do.

It's weird, and nothing like what my friends experience. I'm the only one with this bizarre living arrangement. Some days I wish for just two parents, and maybe a sibling. Being raised by a tribe can be interesting, but it also unsettles me sometimes. I don't really belong to anyone but Annie, and even then, she's my sister. I'm not hers, per se. As much as I'd love to be a Barrett brother, the reality is, I'm not. My last name is Wilson, and unfortunately, it always will be.

I love the people I live with, but that doesn't make me one of them.

The guys have this bond, shared history, secrets they won't talk about when I'm around. Oh yeah, I've tried, but they close up like clams when I walk into a room sometimes. I have picked up that it's got to do with Grandpa Ray and the night he died, but that's all I've figured out.

The one time I asked Michael outright, he told me that some things are best left unsaid and he didn't want to burden me with the truth. Then he kicked into some spiel about how awesome life is and we should focus on that.

I even asked Aunt Nell about it once, but she just shook her head and smiled. "I don't know the whole story myself, but even if I did, it's not my place to tell ya. You need to ask the people directly involved."

Yeah, well, I did that and had zero luck!

Talk about frustrating.

I've had to learn to give up on the whole thing, and whenever the thought pops into my head, I shove it aside before it can fester.

All I know is that I'm part of this unconventional family, but I'll never truly be one of them.

Michael strides out of the kitchen and plops a bowl of oatmeal with raisins and cinnamon in front of me. Oooo— plus dried apricots. Nice. I snatch my spoon and dig in while Michael takes a seat and shares a glance with Deeks before frowning at me.

Oh great. Here it comes.

"Where were you this morning?" His glare intensifies.

I swallow down my oatmeal, missing its deliciousness as I try to come up with a good excuse for why I slept through my alarm. Annie usually wakes me when I do that, but she didn't this morning and now I'm facing judge and jury.

"Sorry, man." I wince. "I didn't hear my alarm."

"Probably because you were up so late messing with your guitar," Deeks murmurs, grabbing two strips of bacon off his plate and eating with his fingers.

I resist the urge to kick him under the table. Arley's sitting there, and I don't want to accidentally catch her foot or leg.

"What? Again? " Michael's frown deepens even more,

and I look away from it. "Dude. Do I have to take that thing off you?"

"No!" I snap. "It's one morning. Give me a break."

"Calving season is less than a month away. I can't just give you a break. We've got a lot of work coming up, and we need your help to prepare. Once those calves are born, you can't afford to miss your alarm."

I grit my teeth and mumble into my oatmeal. "Annie didn't wake me."

"Oh, so it's her fault now? Because she doesn't have a million other better things to do than wake up your lazy ass?"

I hate it when Michael gets annoyed. It hardly ever happens. Usually it's Deeks raving on, but not today.

With a sniff, I disengage and focus on my breakfast, throwing Arley a wink when she catches my eye with a worried frown. She grins at me before licking a smear of plum jam off her cheek.

She's too cute. Even though she's growing up and changing all the time—she's eight now—she'll always be the cutest kid in the world.

Is it weird that I kind of don't want her to grow up too fast?

A thumping on the stairs makes me glance up as Annie comes rushing down. She's looking pale and disheveled this morning, and it only occurs to me now... why didn't she wake me? Is she sick?

She's looking kind of off color as she walks up to the table and stares at Michael with wide eyes.

I tense.

He goes still, like he's bracing himself for one of Annie's explosions.

But instead, her eyes start to glisten and she blurts, "I'm pregnant."

Okay, what the hell?

My spoon clatters onto the table as I gape at my sister, then turn a glare on Michael. "Dude! You knocked up my sister? What is wrong with you?"

Deeks starts laughing, but the sound is quickly cut off when Kena shoots him a "shut up" look across the table.

"Shhh." She dips her head, obviously fighting her own smile.

I growl in my throat, turning my attention back to Annie.

"What am I gonna do?" she frets. "I'm not ready for this. We're not even married, Michael!"

Michael's smile is calm. All the angst he was firing at me has vanished, and Annie would usually swoon at this moment, doing that melty face thing she does and telling Michael how beautiful he is.

Ugh. Gag me.

Michael slowly stands, gently touching Annie's cheek and saying, "Well, we could do something about that."

Annie flicks his hands away. "You can't just marry me because I'm pregnant with your kid."

"No, but I can because I'm completely in love with you."

She goes still, her large eyes glistening in a new way, like she's about to smile.

Her lips twitch, and I know I should be happy about

this exchange right now. They love each other. This is a good thing.

But shit! Annie's pregnant?

She's gonna be having a kid of her own?

"Why aren't you freakin' out about this?" Annie's voice wobbles.

Michael touches her cheek, then lightly runs his hand down her body and rests it against her stomach. "Because, a part of you and a part of me is growing in your belly right now. I think that's kinda cool."

Yep. He's good with words. I have to give him that.

My sister can't fight her tears anymore, her smile growing as the first few slide free from her eyes. "I don't know anything about being a mother."

Michael lets out a soft laugh. "Come on. You're helping raise Arley, and you're the closest thing Jackson's got to a mother. He's turned out, well, you know... okay, I guess."

"Hardy har har." I hope my glare is strong enough to match the heavy sarcasm in my voice.

Michael winks at me like he's funny, but I can't muster a smile right now. I should be going around the table and hugging my sister, telling her how great this is. But I can't seem to do it.

Getting out of my seat, I push my oatmeal away. "I gotta go to school. Arley, am I taking you today, kiddo?"

"Yes, please." She perks up.

"Oh, that would be great. Thanks, Jackson." Kena smiles at me, then looks to Arley.

"Let's get you ready, little one."

Arley shoves in the last of her toast and grabs my hand.

I pause at the base of the stairs and point at Michael, who is still giving Annie gooey eyes. "Don't even think about doing some half-assed proposal over breakfast. My sister deserves better than that."

Michael's eyebrows shoot up in surprise while Deeks starts laughing again. As I take Arley upstairs, I can hear him saying, "He's getting bossier, right? It's not just me who thinks that?"

They all start to laugh, and I shake my head, kind of reeling over the news.

"Oh, Annie. Congratulations, chicky. You're gonna be a mama." Kena's voice carries up the stairs, and I bet the girls are hugging right now.

My sister's pregnant.

Holy crap.

She's going to have a baby of her own. It's like a whole new era. Since Cooper returned home five years ago, things have found this happy rhythm, and now it's all going to change.

Not to sound selfish, but I kind of don't know where that leaves me.

I'm not Annie's kid. I don't belong to anyone here.

And if she and Michael get married, she'll officially become a Barrett... something I can never truly be.

2

TIMING IS EVERYTHING

Hailey

MY SNEAKERS PAD along the concrete path, nerves skittering through me as I fidget with my bag strap and try to come up with different lines I can use.

"I'm really sorry, Jackson, but…"

No. Don't start with an apology. You haven't done anything wrong.

"So, the thing is, I can't go to prom with you anymore."

Ugh! I'm just gonna blurt it out like that?

"You know how we made that deal…"

I shake my head, a groan running through me as I try to figure out how to do this. I've been stressing ever since the prom posters started popping up around school yesterday. It's all come so suddenly, and I'm not sure how to deal with it.

Jackson and I were twelve when we made a deal to go together. That was years ago. Things have changed, and he can't honestly expect me to go through with that promise, right? I mean, we were kids! And it's not like *I* was the one who pushed him away.

He was the one who freaked out when I tried to kiss him, and then he practically ignored me for a month. It was awful. I cried almost every night, thinking I'd lost my best friend, but then we found our way back to each other. It just naturally happened one day when he saw me crying over yet another failed test and he offered to secretly tutor me. I couldn't refuse, and we've been tutor buddies ever since. But never best of best friends like we used to be. Now we just hang with the same group of people and it's all very platonic.

Well, mostly.

I close my eyes against a memory I seriously can't unearth right now.

Jackson and I are better off as friends, which is why going to prom together is a huge mistake. Surely he'll be able to see that.

That's not why you can't go with him!

My mouth twists into a frown while my stomach gurgles with a sour taste that's going to make me trip over my words. I just know it will.

How do I look Jackson in the eye and tell him the deal's off?

I wince and rush to my locker. Maybe if I bury my head deep enough inside it, I won't have to face this dilemma. I managed to avoid him yesterday, but I can already feel the clock ticking.

Tick. Tick. Tick. Tick. Boom!

"Hey, Hails." Jackson greets me like he always does, stopping by my locker and resting his shoulder against the dull metal.

I wince and steal a quick sideways look at him.

That strong jawline, the perfectly straight nose, dark spikes of hair and his...

Hey, where's his standard smile? The one that makes his little dimple show.

Actually, he's looking kind of upset this morning.

Forgetting about my books, I turn to face him. "What's the matter?"

He dips his head, scratching the back of his neck and sighing.

"Jackson, come on. What's wrong?"

"Annie's pregnant," he mumbles.

"What?" I blink in surprise.

He looks up and repeats it slowly. "My sister is pregnant."

"Oh wow. Really?" I can't help a giddy laugh. "That's so exciting."

He grunts, and my laughter disintegrates.

"Hey." I nudge his shoulder lightly with my fist. "It *is* exciting. Babies are cute."

He shrugs.

"Oh come on, you know they are."

"They also cry a lot and poop everywhere." He crosses his arms and scowls at the floor.

"That's not why you're upset." I give him a sympathetic smile. "What's really bugging you?"

"I don't know."

When I probe him with my "knowing" look, he flicks his arm up.

"Seriously! I don't know what's bugging me. I just... I can't believe Annie's gonna have a baby."

His confused annoyance is kinda sweet. I let it slide and try to move the conversation in a more positive direction.

"Are they gonna get married?"

"Yeah, probably."

"Wow. How cool is that? I wonder if they'll have a big wedding like Cooper and Ashlyn."

"Highly unlikely." Jackson shakes his head. "That thing was a freaking carnival."

"Only because Ashlyn's mother and her friend Leo took charge. I'm pretty sure Ashlyn would have happily gotten married in the middle of a field with like two witnesses."

"Come on, she loved it. That dress. Remember her going on and on about the bazillion-dollar dress?"

I giggle at Jackson's eyes roll. "She never told us how much it cost."

"She didn't have to. The thing had diamonds sewn into it."

More giggling. I can't help it. Jackson's cute when he's exasperated. "They weren't real diamonds, and you have to admit that she looked ah-maaaa-zing. Cooper's face when she walked down the aisle…" I let out a dreamy sigh. The love radiating from him was enough to light the Empire State Building.

Jackson grunts and I blink, schooling my expression so he doesn't think I'm some romantic sap.

With a casual shrug, I close my locker. "We got to fly to New York. I mean, that was cool. I still can't believe they invited me."

"Why?" Jackson's head pops up, his expression complete bafflement.

I shrug. "I don't know. I'm not family."

Jackson gives me a sad smile and opens his mouth but doesn't say anything.

I can feel the awkward train pulling into the station and quickly start talking. "It's still the most stunning wedding I've ever seen, and I bet the only couple to top it will be Indy and Brody, because her dad's, like, loaded and will give her whatever she wants."

"They're not even engaged."

"But they're living together. It's only a matter of time."

Jackson closes his eyes like he doesn't want to think about it. I know him well enough to understand how much he hates change. That's what's bugging him about Annie's news. Another huge change. His life has been filled with constant ups and downs. Each disruption unsettles him for a bit until he can adjust. That's just Jackson's way.

Maybe telling him about the prom thing today is a really bad idea. I think I'll just let Annie's news ride for a while, then casually pop it into a conversation somewhere down the line. I can't dump one more upset in his lap. That's just cruel.

Hopefully he'll be too distracted by his sister's bombshell to even think about prom anyway.

I've got time to figure out how to tell him the real reason I can't go.

And man, am I grateful for every minute of it.

3

_____

HOW TO PROPOSE

MICHAEL ADJUSTS the gloves on his hands, pausing for a moment to think about Annie's words just that morning. The vulnerable look on her face, the way her lips quivered as she tried to get a read on him. It made his heart do funny things. Things only she could ever do to him.

He loves her. With every fiber of his being.

And now they're going to have a baby together. He's going to be a dad!

He should be terrified, but the joy bursting through him is a pleasant surprise. He's never really taken the time to think about parenthood. Things on the ranch are always so busy, and life has just kind of trundled along without him really noticing. Sure, he's thought about his future with Annie on a daydream, but they've never discussed next steps. All that stuff has always been pushed back as they hit a new season or prepared for another change within the family.

But Annie's little announcement this morning is

forcing their hands, and Michael is surprisingly happy about it.

A smile toys with his lips as he clears out a space in the barn to prepare for calving. Life on the ranch is about to get real busy, and the more preparation they can do in advance, the better.

His brothers will be arriving soon to help. Hopefully they can get most of the job done before lunch.

"Proposal," he whispers to himself, wondering how he's going to do it.

The look on Jackson's face was pretty clear. He's not allowed to screw this up. Annie deserves the best kind of proposal he can give her. The kid's right. Nothing half-assed.

Michael's brow creases as he thinks about Jackson's reaction this morning. He seemed kind of grumpy about the whole thing.

Why?

Shouldn't he be happy for his sister? For him?

He's going to be an uncle. That's pretty cool.

The loyalty between Jackson and Annie is fierce, and although Michael thinks of Jackson like his own flesh and blood, he's technically not.

I wonder if he's stressed about things changing with us having a baby. Annie will be distracted with motherhood.

Michael makes a mental note to catch up with Jackson after school, maybe have a heart-to-heart and figure out what's going on in his head. The fact that he slept in this morning was odd. Maybe something else is going on and Jackson just needs a chance to open up about it.

Walking out of the barn, Michael goes to grab the fencing to use as sectioning for the calves when he sees it being carried toward him. Brody and Cooper have arrived and are already kicking into work mode.

Michael grins at his brothers, wondering when he's going to tell them about what happened over breakfast. Now that Brody and Indy live together in Harborton, they're not around as much. And as soon as Cooper and Ashlyn got married, they moved up to the house they had built over the summer. It's still on the ranch, but it's half a mile from the main house, nestled on the edge of the forest and overlooking the valley below. You can't see it from the main house, and it gives the couple the privacy they want.

When they first proposed the plan, Michael was kind of offended, but Annie helped him realize that four couples living in the ranch house was too much. She was right, of course. Even with the six of them in there, it feels kind of full and busy some days. Jackson is only getting bigger, growing into a full-fledged man, and Arley, although she's small, can be freaking loud when she wants to be.

Taking half of Deeks's load, Michael walks into the barn and rests it against the thick wooden beam. Brody and Cooper get to work, oblivious to the huge change coming their way.

I should tell them. Just blurt it out. But where do I start?

"So, did you guys hear Michael's gonna be a papa bear?"

Everyone goes still, the sudden silence in the barn oppressive.

Michael throws a glare over his shoulder, but Deeks just meets it with a happy grin and a wink.

"What are you talking about?" Brody finally asks.

Deeks's smile grows a little wider. "In about what? Eight months would you say?"

Brody's still looking confused, while Cooper pings straight and blinks a couple times.

"Annie's pregnant?" he asks.

All Michael can do is catch his brother's eye and nod.

"No way." Brody whoops, dropping the fencing and engulfing Michael in one of his famous bear hugs. "That's awesome! Congratulations!" He lifts Michael off his feet and cheers again.

"Yeah, yeah. Okay. Okay. Put me down." He pats Brody's shoulder and can't help a short laugh.

It is good news. It's freaking great news.

And Brody's reaction is making him realize how bummed out he is that Jackson didn't respond the same way.

"What's the matter? Why are you frowning?" Cooper's steady gaze, which always sees everything, makes Michael sigh.

"I don't know. I mean, I'm stoked. I just…" Michael whips off his glove, running a hand through his hair. "Annie's kind of scared and overwhelmed by the whole thing, and then Jackson—"

"Acted like a total douche about it," Deeks finishes for him.

Michael frowns but doesn't deny the truth. Jackson's reaction *was* kinda douchey.

"Ah, so he's not excited about his sister getting knocked up." Brody brushes it off. "I wouldn't worry about it. He's a teenager. The last thing he wants to think about is you doing his sister." Michael glares at Brody, but his bigger brother is oblivious as he keeps going. "He's probably grossed out."

Deeks starts laughing. "He was pretty clear that Michael wasn't allowed to propose right then and there, either."

Cooper grins. "Nice. Another wedding to look forward to. Are you going to try and get married before the baby comes?"

"I haven't even proposed yet." Michael shoves his gloves back on and gets back to work.

"So, how're you gonna ask her?" Cooper helps him with the fencing while Deeks and Brody work on the section behind them.

"I have no idea. How did you ask again?"

"Mine was super simple. Ashlyn and I were hanging out in a spot in the woods. That little swimming hole we love so much. The sun was hitting her skin, and the smile on her face... oh man, I couldn't wait. The question just popped out of me. I didn't even have a ring, but she said yes, and we went shopping that weekend."

Michael contemplates that for a moment, picturing the scene before shaking his head. "I think I want to have the ring on me."

"Fair enough. Guess you'll have to fit in a trip to town

sometime soon, then. Not that there's a great selection there. You'll have way more choice if you drive to Missoula."

"Yeah." Michael lets out a nervous laugh, the pressure of the ultimate proposal weighing on him.

Maybe Brody would have a good idea. He's a total romantic.

"What do you think, Bro?"

"About what?" He clears his throat.

"About proposing. When you eventually ask Indy, how are you gonna do it?"

Michael turns in time to see Brody's jaw clench before he pastes on a fake look of confusion and murmurs, "Sorry, what'd you say?"

Michael's eyes narrow and he crosses his arms, watching the youngest Barrett boy carefully. "When you propose. How are you gonna do it?"

Brody shrugs. "I dunno."

"Yeah right." Deeks shakes his head. "The most romantic guy on the planet hasn't thought about it? Whatever, you big liar."

"You are going to marry Indy eventually, right?" Cooper wipes his arm across his forehead. "You can't just keep living together forever."

Before Brody can answer, Deeks asks, "Why not?" He pauses to frown. "What's wrong with that?"

Cooper glances at him. "You never want to get married?"

Deeks shrugs. "I just don't feel like I need it."

"What does Kena think about that?"

"Not sure. I've never asked her."

"Well, maybe you should." Cooper's pointed look makes Deeks's eyebrows pinch together.

"You think she'll want to? Aw, man, I don't want to go through some wedding hoopla."

"Why not? It's fun." Cooper grins.

"Fun? You call New York fun?"

Cooper's smile grows into a laugh. "As long as I stayed out of the way and did whatever Leo told me to, it was fine."

Deeks makes a face, and they all start laughing.

"You don't have to have a big, fussy wedding like those two did," Brody interjects. "You could go to city hall, for crying out loud."

"Yeah, like you and Indy will do that." Deeks laughs. "Your wedding will be more elaborate than Cooper's."

"No it won't."

"Yeah, right."

"It won't."

"Gimme a break. It totally will."

"It won't." Brody's adamant response has Michael pausing in his work yet again.

"It will!" Deeks spits back, never one to lose a fight.

"It won't."

"It will!"

Brody shakes his head, obviously annoyed that Deeks won't drop this. "It won't. It can't."

"Why not?"

"Because we're already married!" Brody's sharp admission makes them all freeze.

Brody gapes at the ground while everyone else stares at him and doesn't know what to say, until Deeks finally explodes.

"What!"

Brody winces and rubs his forehead. "Indy and I got married in Vegas last year."

"I thought that was a weekend getaway!" Deeks barks.

"It was."

"But you went there to get married?"

"That wasn't the initial plan, but while we were there, we thought, why not? It keeps it out of the public eye, just a quiet service, and no one has to know."

"Including your family?" Deeks barks. "What the hell, Brody!"

"I..." He sighs.

"How could you not tell us this!"

"We were going to when we got back home, but then we felt kind of bad for not including you, so we didn't say anything, and then every time we've gone to mention it, something else comes up, and now too much time has passed. It's just awkward."

"You guys are unbelievable!" Deeks goes back to work, his huffs and sharp movements making it clear to everyone how pissed he is.

Cooper and Michael share a quick look before quietly returning to work as well.

Michael keeps stealing glances at Brody, wondering if the guy missed out or is actually one lucky man. No wedding prep or stress? Sounds kinda nice.

But Annie deserves more than that. She deserves the pretty dress and the flowers. She deserves a proposal that will sweep her right off her feet.

He has no idea the kind of wedding Annie's dreamed of, but he wants to give it to her. He wants to do this right. They've been living together for five years; he knows what's important to her. Which means he needs to talk to someone first, before he can make any of Annie's dreams come true.

4

RESPECT

Jackson

HAILEY'S BEEN ACTING weird all day, and I can't figure out why. I need to ask her about prom, but every time I went to today, it's like she knew what I was about to say and quickly filled in the space before I could talk. We hung out with our usual crowd at lunchtime, stealing food off each other's trays and laughing while we joked about Mr. Hensley's lame story in biology and the fact that Mrs. Wheedler was wearing two different shoes, but no one had the heart to tell her. I tried to enjoy it but spent the whole time stressing over why Hailey was avoiding me. She wouldn't even make eye contact across the table. She even canceled our tutoring session this afternoon, which is why I called Kena and offered to get Arley after school.

Pulling the pickup truck to the curb, I cut the engine and grin at the sea of children running around out the front of school. Arley had to wait for me, but I can see her happily playing with her friends—a mix of boys and girls climbing all over the jungle gym while a couple mothers hover nearby, chatting and sipping coffee from takeout cups. One of them holds a stroller, pushing it back and forth on autopilot while she listens to her friend.

Shit. That's gonna be Annie soon.

Arley was two by the time Kena and Deeks got to the ranch. It'll be weird having a crying, pooping baby in the house. I've never been around that kind of thing before. I guess it'll be a big change for all of us.

Thoughts of my petite sister with a round basketball belly make me frown, and I push the door open before I can think about it anymore.

"Arley!" I shout across the lawn, raising my hand when she spins to see me. Her pigtails, which are falling out and messy, flip around her face. Scrambling down the equipment, she jumps off the last rung of the ladder and hurtles toward me.

Even though she's eight now, she still likes to hug me the way she always has, full torpedo launch into my arms, and I swing her around a couple times.

Her giggles make me smile, and her legs propel into the air as I dance her around one, two, three times, then drop her back to her feet.

"Hey, Jack Jack."

"How was school?"

"Fun!" She jumps on her toes, then grabs my hand and starts walking for the gate.

"You got your backpack?"

"Oh!" She gasps and races back to the playground, waving goodbye to her friends as she hitches the bag on her shoulder and runs back to me. I wave at the two mothers, calling out, "Thanks for watching her."

They grin and smile while Arley slips her hand into mine and starts skipping for the truck.

"I told everyone that I'm going to be a big sister! They were super excited. I'm kinda hoping that Annie might let me name the baby, because I told Erica Mattley that she was gonna let me." She winces, and even though I want to laugh at her cute expression, I force a frown. "I know!" she cries. "It just slipped out, and then she was so excited about it, I couldn't take it back."

Okay, too cute.

I crack up laughing as I help her into the truck and make sure she's buckled safely.

"Can you not tell Annie I said that?"

"Why don't you just ask her if she'll let you give her some suggestions?"

"Do you think she'll mind?"

"Nope." I shake my head and saunter around the truck, thinking about what Arley said.

Big sister.

It's not actually true, but I don't have the heart to tell her that she and Annie aren't related, and she'll never actually be someone's sister. Unless Kena and

Deeks have kids, but even then, Arley is kind of adopted.

That still counts! I reprimand myself as I slip into the vehicle. I'm an orphan too and no one adopted me, although I've always felt like Annie's brother-son, in some ways. I definitely won't be once the baby's born. So what does that make me?

This whole setup at the Barrett ranch is getting to me more than usual.

Cooper and Ashlyn have built a house up on the ridge, so they're not living in the ranch house anymore, and Brody and Indy live in town. But the house still feels crowded sometimes, and if everyone starts having babies, it's just gonna get worse. I'll be pushed further and further into the background until there's no place left at all.

Maybe they're expecting me to leave and head off to college, but I kinda want to stay and work the ranch with them. If they'll let me.

Maybe they won't.

Maybe there's no space for me.

The thought sits heavy and dark in my gut, and I don't say much as I drive Arley home. She prattles on about her school day, everything from Aaron McBride's boogers to Lanxin Cho's new red skirt.

I nod and "hmmm" the way I'm supposed to, and she doesn't even notice how little attention I'm paying to her. I would feel guilty about not being so attentive, but I've got a lot on my mind right now.

We pull up to the house, and Arley jumps out, racing

around the truck to greet Michael as he lopes down the stairs.

"Hey, Mikey!" She jumps into his arms, scores a kiss on the cheek, and then rushes inside. "I'm starving!"

That's her standard "hello" at the end of a busy school day.

Michael chuckles and walks toward me, pushing up his sleeves and suddenly looking serious.

Oh crap. He's gonna tell me off about sleeping in this morning, or maybe for yelling at him at the breakfast table.

Michael's not as scary as my sister when he gets mad, but that quiet, frosty disappointment is the worst. I take in a full breath, readying myself with excuses.

"Can we talk for a minute?"

"I've kind of got homework."

"It won't take long." Michael smiles at me, and that's even more unnerving. What's he playing at?

With a thick swallow, I grip my bag strap and follow him to the fence line. He rests his forearm on a post and stares out at the view while I shuffle from foot to foot beside him.

"So, how was school?" His voice is a little tight, and I can tell he really doesn't care about my answer to that question.

"Dude." I snicker. "Just get on with it. Is it about this morning?"

"Yeah." Michael sighs and rubs the back of his neck.

I open my mouth to apologize but then wait a beat,

wondering what I should be apologizing for. Do I just list it out?

Sorry for sleeping in.

Sorry for yelling at you after Annie's announcement.

Sorry for stomping up the stairs and acting like a brat.

But *am* I sorry for any of that stuff?

I mean, the sleeping in was a legit mistake, but I am kind of annoyed that he just knocked her up and she's all panicked. It's great that he loves her and all, but—

"Okay, fine." He nods. "I wanted to ask if you'd give me permission to marry Annie."

I blink and have to repeat his words in my head, just to really make sure I understand them.

He's asking my permission?

"Her dad doesn't want to acknowledge his part in her life, and although her grandparents check in occasionally, the only really solid person in her family that she adores the most is you. And I don't want to go asking her to marry me if you really hate that idea. I mean, I guess I'm going to ask her no matter what you think, but I really, *really* want you to be happy about it."

"You're asking for my blessing?" I tap my chest, still struggling to speak properly.

His smile is slow to form, reaching his eyes before his lips. "Yeah. It's important to me."

"Wow." I take a step back, shoving my hands in my pockets and blinking at the mountains in the distance. "I mean, yeah. Of course. I'm pretty sure Annie would kill me if I said no."

Michael laughs and pats my shoulder before giving it a

squeeze. "This conversation is just between you and me. Would you be cool if I ask Annie to marry me?"

He looks me in the eye, and I couldn't refuse him if I tried.

This guy is a good man, and I want Annie to be happy.

With a grin, I bob my head and say, "Of course. You guys are meant for each other. Of course I want you to get married."

"Awesome." Michael's grin is sweet, maybe a little nervous.

I snicker and slap his arm. "You know how you're gonna ask her yet?"

He shakes his head. "No idea. I want it to be so special, but I'm not the most creative guy in the world. I'm not sure what I'm gonna do."

"You'll figure it out."

"Yeah." He nods. "Hopefully."

"Just make sure it's authentic. That's all that really matters."

Michael grins. "I like that."

I'm feeling just a little puffed with... I don't know, a good feeling, I guess. Michael respects me enough to make sure I'm all good with the whole marriage thing. That's kinda cool. I bury my hands in my jacket pockets and try to figure out what to say next. We both go quiet for a minute, the world still and peaceful around us.

"So, how was school today?" Michael eventually asks. "I genuinely want to know."

I grin at my future brother-in-law and shake my head. After just saying yes to his question, I can't exactly go into the fact that this whole pregnancy/marriage thing has got me majorly rattled.

But I feel like a flippant "Yeah, good" won't fly either.

So I go for the other thing that's been eating me up today. "It was… weird."

"What do you mean?" Michael's genuine concern makes it easy to confess.

I scratch the back of my neck and tell him about Hailey and how she was kind of avoiding me today.

"Do you think she's upset with you over something?"

"I don't think so. She was friendly this morning. Nothing seemed that off. Maybe she's upset because I haven't asked her to prom yet?"

"You're gonna do that?" Michael's eyes light with a smile.

"Well, only because we made a deal ages ago that we'd go together."

"So, what are you waiting for, then?"

"Yeah. I know. I mean, I tried to find my chance today, but she kept on dodging me. Maybe she doesn't want to go with me anymore."

Michael gives me a sad smile and nods. "Maybe."

My shoulders slump.

He chuckles. "Or she might say yes." He winks and grins at me. "You'll never know unless you ask, right? You just gotta go for it."

"Michael! Let's go!" Deeks waves his arm, beckoning him down the road toward the barn.

"Do you need my help?" I ask.

"Nah, you said you've got homework, right? Get that out of the way and you can help me in the morning."

"I promise to set a second alarm this time."

He chuckles, lightly slapping my shoulder before running to catch up with Deeks.

I watch them go, thinking about what he said and pulling out my phone before I can change my mind.

Hey, Hails. Can we talk tomorrow? I kind of want to ask you something.

The text turns blue, telling me it's been delivered, and I tap my thumb on my phone screen, hoping to see the message change to Read and then those little gray dots that indicate she's sending a reply.

But after a few moments of waiting, I've still got nothing.

She must be busy, doing whatever it is that made her cancel tutoring.

With a sigh, I shove the phone in my back pocket and head inside. I guess I may as well distract myself with homework.

Oh joy.

5

MY FIRST BOYFRIEND

Hailey

MY PHONE DINGS AGAIN, reminding me that there's a message on my screen that I should probably check. It could be Mom or Aunt Joy wondering where I am.

"One sec," I breathe, pulling away to grab my phone.

The second I scan the screen, my heart plummets.

Jackson wants to talk.

Crap!

"Who's that?" A silky voice against my ear makes me fumble the phone. I tuck it under my leg and turn back to the guy who's got me all distracted. The new guy in town, the one who's starting over and making me a part of his new adventure—Josh DeLancey.

I grin at him, running my fingers down his cheek. "It's no one. Just a friend from school."

Like I'm gonna tell him about Jackson, the most confusing person in my life.

"Hopefully not a boyfriend." Josh grins.

"Of course not." I laugh, trying to hide the pinching in my gut.

I wanted him to be. For so long, I wanted Jackson Wilson to be all mine, but...

Josh's lips distract me from the rest of that thought. They're full, his mouth a warm oasis that my tongue just loves to play in.

I've never really had a boyfriend before. Not one who sneaks me to the lake so we can make out after school. We come here as much as we can, this private little spot hidden among the trees. Josh gets half an hour off work in the afternoon, and he always meets me right after school so we can share this bliss before he has to get back to the garage where he's training to become a mechanic.

His grease monkey hand doesn't bother me as it skims my thigh, my waist, my lower back before curving beneath my butt. His other hand rests lightly on my neck as he sends me to another planet with his intoxicating mouth.

I still can't believe we're together. I wouldn't call Josh my usual type. We met at a party just outside of town. I didn't really want to go, but Petra and Tash were set on the idea. They wanted a girls' night out and were trying to convince me and Simone to loosen up already and join them. We caved to peer pressure, and I regretted it the second we walked into a house I'd never been to before. It was loud and chaotic, smoke swirling through the air, alcohol flowing freely and some other substances that explained the wild behavior going on in the kitchen and over by the trampoline.

I held Simone's hand until she abandoned me to get a drink, and I swear I nearly bailed. I was minutes away from running outside and putting in an SOS to Jackson. He would have come for me without any explanation required.

But then Josh appeared. He could obviously sense how nervous I was, because he studied me for a moment, and then his face puckered with concern.

"Hey, are you okay?"

To my humiliation, my eyes glassed with tears. He gently laid his hand on my lower back and coaxed the truth out of me.

"I don't usually come to parties like this. I guess I'm kind of overwhelmed."

"Hey. You don't have to worry. I'll look after you." His smile was so kind, his eyes telling me I was safe, so I stayed by his side for the rest of the party. We talked until my friends had to drag me away.

"My dad will kill me if I get home after one!" It was Petra's plea that finally pulled me loose, but not before giving Josh my number.

I floated home that night. I'd given this cute, sweet guy my number!

Would he call?

Would he text?

Was that just *one* magical night?

It wasn't.

He called!!

The next day, he got in touch to check on me, and then the day after that, we stayed up until the early hours of the morning texting each other. This whirlwind romance has swept me right off my feet.

I guess sometimes it scares me a little. But it also thrills me.

I've kept Josh a secret from everyone but Petra, Tash, and Simone. They all think it's totally romantic, and the fact that it's a secret makes it even better. They've been amazing, not breathing a word to anyone and playing it totally cool at school as well. I give them updates over the phone, and it's like we've formed this secret little club away from the guys. It's brought us closer together, which is nice.

With their help, the whole secret-keeping thing is way easier. I'm not overly keen on telling Mom, Aunt Joy, or Mom's new husband, Richard. I also don't want to tell Dad or his girlfriend. I can't imagine any of them loving the fact that I'm dating a nineteen-year-old. It's only a three-year age gap, so not a big deal, really, but he's definitely not the type my parents would want me with. He's got a bad-boy edge, an attitude, a swagger. He's the kind of guy you don't bring home to dinner, and I can't even place exactly why. I just know they wouldn't like him.

Josh groans, deepening the kiss until I feel like I can't breathe. I drown for a few seconds more, then pull away to catch my breath, lightly guiding his hand out from under my shirt.

We haven't gone all the way yet. I can tell Josh really wants to. I mean, he hasn't said that, but the look in his eyes and the way his hands like to wander tell me enough.

Maybe I'll be ready soon. I'm not sure exactly what's holding me back, I just… well, we haven't even been dating a month. It's not like we've said the L-word or really confessed our feelings for each other. Plus, he'll be my first.

I don't know if I want to lose my virginity in his car by the lake.

That's not exactly how I pictured it happening.

Forbidden thoughts that I haven't entertained in a while scuttle through me, and Josh is definitely not a part of them.

Jackson.

My insides flush and I try to school my expression, hoping Josh can't read my mind. I should *not* be thinking of Jackson in that way… or at all! I'm with my boyfriend right now.

Josh studies my face, running his fingers down my cheek like he's trying to memorize the shape. I bite my lips together, nerves sizzling my stomach.

"What is it?"

"Nothing. I just…" I brush my finger down the edge of my phone, which is still wedged under my leg.

Josh's eyes narrow in that concerned way of his. "Who was the text from? Is everything okay?"

"Yeah, I…"

How much do I say?

I lick my lips and reprimand my hesitancy.

He's your boyfriend! Tell him the truth!

"Well, the thing is… my prom's coming up, and I was…"

"Oh man, I'd love to go with you." His smile grows a little wider.

I giggle. It sounds stupid, but I can't help it. He wants to go with me!

Jackson. You were supposed to go with Jackson.

The smile slips off my face and I glance out the windshield.

"I never made it to prom," Josh murmurs. "It'd be fun to take you, but…"

I glance back, wondering where he's going with this. He winces. "I'm not sure it's a great idea. I kind of like how we're keeping our relationship under wraps, you know? Prom will just put us right in the spotlight, and…" He gently skims his fingers down my cheek. "What do you think?"

"You're probably right."

"Aw, don't be sad." He puts on a fake pout, then grins and winks at me. "Hey, I know. Why don't you bail and I'll take you out for a special night instead? We could drive out of town and do… I don't know. I'll think of something cool."

"Bail on prom?" I bite my lip, not sure how to feel about that. The idea of all that time with Josh is pretty appealing. But do I honestly not want to go to prom with my friends? "Yeah, maybe." Is my smile too tight?

"We could have fun, Hailey Parker. I could show you a

really good time." He wiggles his eyebrows, making me blush.

I dip my head, nodding in agreement, but he sees right through me.

"Hey, what's wrong? I can tell you want to say yes, but you also don't. Is prom that important to you?"

I shrug. "I guess I just always thought I'd go, and…" After a short sigh, I blurt the truth. "Thing is… I made a deal with one of my friends years ago that we'd go together."

"Which friend?"

"His name's Jackson, and we've been buddies since we were kids. We always said we'd go to our first prom together."

Josh's dark eyebrows wrinkle with a frown. "Well, you'll have to tell him you can't."

"But how, when I'm keeping you a secret?"

"You'll just have to come up with an excuse. Or tell him you want to go with a big group, like all your friends together."

I nod, knowing that won't fly. I can't even explain how I know that. I just do.

"If I can't convince you to spend prom with me, than at least promise me you'll go with all your friends and not just this Jackson guy. It'll feel too much like a date, and that will drive me crazy, knowing you're hanging out with someone else."

I steal a glance at his face. His voice is getting kinda tight. But when he catches my eye, he grins and leans in for a kiss. "You're my girl."

He runs his fingertips over my skin again, and then he's drawing me in for another kiss. I can't resist him. As I sink into his arms, I try to switch off my chaotic brain.

The thought that I'm Josh's girl thrills me, but then it crashes into the thought of having to let Jackson down.

I'll definitely push the friends thing, but I'll have to have a good reason why.

Maybe I should just tell him about Josh.

Jackson will understand, right? He's a reasonable guy, and I can trust him with this secret. Telling him the truth will be better than trying to fudge my way through a lie.

Besides, we made that deal years ago, and I wasn't the one who ruined our chances of becoming a couple. Jackson was the first to pull away; I'm only safeguarding myself against a pain like that again.

We're better off as just friends, which means I shouldn't feel guilty about being loyal to my legit boyfriend.

6

THREE PHONE CALLS IN A ROW

JAKE KNOWS he's supposed to be working on a paper right now, but Carmen was right there, and when she leaned her head against his shoulder and smelled so dang good, he couldn't resist. Within moments they were lying on the couch, her safely tucked beneath him while they made out like horny teenagers.

He wouldn't have it any other way.

As his lips nibble her neck, he runs his hands over the perfect shape of her body and is overcome with gratitude.

This woman is perfect.

This moment is perfect.

This—

His phone starts ringing.

Perfection shattered.

With an irritated grunt, he ignores whoever is calling him and continues to explore the shape of Carmen's jawline with his lips.

She doesn't seem to mind ignoring the call either, her pleasant moans sending rockets of pleasure firing through him.

And the phone starts ringing again.

Carmen giggles against his cheek. "Do you think we should answer that?"

"Voice mail was invented for a reason," Jake murmurs between kisses, capturing her mouth and falling into the bliss that is Carmen Díaz.

When the phone starts ringing a third time, Jake lets out a groan while Carmen stretches out to the coffee table and checks the screen.

"It's Deeks."

Jake rolls his eyes. "We can definitely ignore that. He's just being a pain in the ass."

Carmen shakes her head with a grin and answers it anyway, putting it on speaker so they can stay locked within their tangle of limbs.

He rests his forehead against hers and greets his brother with a "This better be good."

"Hey, buddy! Hope I'm not disturbing you."

"Yeah, right!" Jake rolls his eyes.

Deeks lets out a hard laugh, then turns serious, his tone changing so fast it's like whiplash. "This is important."

Jake looks at the phone, his eyes narrowing on the device. "What's the matter?"

"Did you know Brody was married?"

Jake's eyes bulge and he whips a look at Carmen, whose cheeks are turning pink with embarrassment.

They share an awkward wince.

"Ah…" Jake's not sure what to say.

"You did! You little shit! How could you not tell us!"

"Brody made me promise not to say anything until he was ready."

"I can't believe he did that. We're freaking family! Finally together again, and he goes off and secretly gets married."

Carmen cringes and leans toward the speaker. "After Ashlyn's wedding, Indy was getting stressed about having to do something similar. You know, her father being a famous billionaire and all."

"I know who her father is!"

"Then you'll understand why she wanted to do something quiet and away from media attention."

Deeks huffs. "I don't care that they got married without us there."

"Yes you do," Jake counters.

"Okay, fine. I do. But I'm more pissed off that they didn't tell us about it!"

Jake squeezes the back of his neck, feeling a little guilty. Brody called him about five minutes after the ceremony, totally buzzing. Jake couldn't believe his brother had been so spontaneous, but then he could… because he's Brody.

After surprised congratulations and laughter, Brody ended the call, and Jake didn't feel like it was his news to pass on. He assumed Brody would tell everyone when they got back to Harborton, and it wasn't until he and

Carmen flew up there that Brody whispered in his ear to keep the marriage a secret.

They don't even wear wedding rings, just matching necklaces that are often hidden away beneath their clothing.

"Well, I guess you know now. He must have said something to you."

"Yeah, it came up, but not by choice. Michael was asking for proposal ideas and—"

"Wait. Michael's going to propose?" Carmen's face lights like the sun before she glances at her own diamond ring with a dreamy smile.

"Yeah, Annie's pregnant."

"She's what?" Jake's eyebrows shoot high.

"Pregnant. And Michael wants to marry her before the baby comes."

"Oh my gosh, that's so exciting!" Carmen swoons. "We'll all be married soon at this rate."

Deeks huffs. "You guys haven't set a date yet, have you?"

"The summer after we finish our master's degrees. That's the closest we have to a date, although Carmen's mother is already researching venues." Jake grins at his bride-to-be. Planning this wedding with her mother will be a test of patience. That woman knows what she wants, but Jake's determined to protect Carmen and make sure the day is everything she dreamed it would be.

Threading their fingers together, they gaze down at each other, momentarily forgetting that Deeks is still on the line.

"I love you," Carmen whispers, lightly kissing him until a little throat clearing pulls them apart.

"Yeah, still here, guys."

"Sorry." Carmen giggles while Deeks huffs yet again.

"What's up, man?" Jake stares at his phone, suddenly wishing for FaceTime so he can see what Deeks's face is doing.

"Nothing," Deeks mutters, then sighs. "Do girls always want you to ask?"

Carmen and Jake share a worried frown before Jake leans toward the coffee table. "You don't want to marry Kena?"

"It's not like that. I mean, she's the only girl I want to be with. I just don't feel like I need marriage. I don't need some ring or a piece of paper. That won't change my love for her."

"Well, maybe she feels the same way. I guess you won't know until you ask."

"Yeah, I guess not." Deeks clears his throat again. "So why is asking that kind of thing so freaking hard?"

Jake grins at Carmen. "You can do it, man. We're Barrett boys. We can do anything."

Deeks snickers, and Jake can picture him shaking his head. "Okay, I'll catch you guys later."

"See ya, man." Jake ends the call, turning to gaze down at his beautiful fiancée.

Lightly touching his face, Carmen whispers, "Were you scared asking me?"

"Not for a second." He grins. "It was the easiest thing in the world. I love you so much, *mi vida*. You're my heart and soul, the only woman I'm meant to be with, and I can't wait to marry you."

Her eyes start to glisten, her expression turning gooey as she reaches for his lips and restarts the session Deeks interrupted.

7

NOT THE RIGHT ANSWER

Jackson

HAILEY NEVER REPLIED to my text, which unnerves me. I'm jittery as I head to our tutoring session this afternoon. We always meet in the library, back corner, away from prying eyes. Hailey never wants people to know how much she struggles with reading and writing. I've helped her as much as I can, and her last English assignment scored a B-, which was a huge victory for her.

Learning comes easy for me, and I've always felt a little bad when she struggles her way through it. Words just don't compute the same way for her as they do for me. She's way better at art and design. Her cake decorating skills are off the charts, and her drawings are phenomenal.

I often have to remind her that it's not like she wants a job that will involve thousands of words. There are so many things she could do with her life. She just has to get through school, and college, if she decides to go.

We talk about it sometimes. The idea of taking the SATs and then trying to get into a college somewhere freaks her out big-time. Thankfully, she doesn't mind the idea of working at her aunt Joy's cupcake shop or setting up a cake decorating business. She doesn't need college to do that.

I'm not sure what I'm gonna do yet.

The idea of college bores me. I'd much rather finish school and start working at the ranch full-time, but Annie is not happy about that idea.

Needless to stay, we're still in *discussions* about it.

But at the end of the day, it's my life, and she's not my mother.

The thought of her becoming an actual mother sits uncomfortably in my stomach, and I hitch my bag onto my shoulder and head through the nonfiction section toward the back corner.

I see Hailey before she sees me and stop for a moment to watch her. She's sitting at the table, the sun from the high window above her casting a soft light over her golden hair. It makes it kind of glow, and I can't help staring. She's getting prettier every year. Gone is the round-faced cherub I first met in Joyous Cupcakes. Her whole face has changed, getting longer and more defined. Her cheekbones are higher, and the makeup she's started wearing makes her eyes brighter and wider. I don't know how that works, but I kinda like it. I mean, she's gorgeous without makeup too. No matter what she paints on her lips, her smile will still be a heart-stopper.

Damn, why didn't I let those lips touch mine when she wanted me to?

Why the hell did I pull away?

Because you were like twelve and you'd never kissed a girl and Hailey was your best friend and it was weird!

I'd never touched lips with anyone before, let alone my best friend.

After a month of basically no talking, I got over myself and we became friends again, and then I had to go and blow it last year.

My feelings have been building for a while, I guess. I didn't want to make a move and ruin anything, but we'd been laughing together after a tutoring session, and she looked so beautiful. I couldn't resist. Without a word, I held her face and leaned in.

And she said, "I don't think this is a good idea."

Talk about a mood killer.

I opened my eyes, and her expression made me let her go real fast. Her smile was apologetic as she shook her head and gave me the "We're so much better off as friends" speech.

"We'll still do prom though, right? Like we always said we would?"

She looked down but nodded. "Yeah, I guess."

It wasn't exactly the response I wanted, but I was going to hold her to it.

Maybe I can prove how much I care, show her that we

could be so much more than buddies. I'll buy her a nice corsage, give her an evening to remember, show her that I can be a perfect gentleman, a guy worth dating.

Hope soars in my chest, images making me step forward with a grin. But everything fades the second she glances up and sees me.

Her expression flashes with a frown, and then she's casting her gaze away from me. Just like she did yesterday and all day today.

I pretend not to notice, pulling out a chair and taking a seat beside her. "Hey."

I want to play it cool, casual, but it's kind of hard when she's acting all edgy.

"Hi." She bobs her head, then bites her lips together and pulls over her study binder. "So today I thought we could go over—"

"Do you mind if I ask you something first?"

Her forehead crinkles, but she nods. "Uh... I suppose so."

My heart is beating like a freaking bass drum as I swivel in my seat so my body is angled toward her. She stays straight in her chair, staring at the desk, and for a second I nearly say, "Don't worry about it."

But I can't!

I can't keep pretending that something's not right between us.

"Hailey." I hold my breath, the words suddenly crammed inside my mouth like too much popcorn.

Like that time we had a movie night at her place and

got bored with the TV and started playing "Who can fit the most food into their mouth?"

It was the best.

The memory of Hailey's laughter as she spat popcorn all over my shirt makes me grin, and I take her hand without thinking. Her long fingers are so smooth and perfect. I gaze down at them, running my thumb over the shiny purple polish with a smile.

"Hailey, will you go to prom with me?"

She swallows, staring at our connection before gently pulling her fingers out of my grasp and ruining everything with a soft "No."

8

MY FIRST CRUSH VS. MY FIRST BOYFRIEND

Hailey

THE CRESTFALLEN LOOK on Jackson's face just about kills me, and I rush to explain, not really taking the time to think my words through. I just need him to understand. To not be sad.

"I know we made a deal and everything, but that was years ago, and things have changed."

"But they don't have to change. I mean, I know I screwed up with the whole kissing thing, and I will regret it forever, but—"

"It's not that." I shake my head, hyperaware of his phrasing. He thinks he screwed up? He'll regret it forever? What does that mean?

It doesn't matter what it means. You have Josh now.

But which kiss is he talking about? The one I tried to give him or the one he tried to give me?

Because if it's the latter, I have kicked myself so many times for not letting him lay those gorgeous lips on mine. I'd dreamed about it for years, and then he finally goes to do it and I get scared and give him the friends speech. I mean, honestly!

Hey! You have Josh now!

My swallow is thick, and I quickly lick my lips before trying to fix this. "I mean, it's not like a total no. I just mean we can't go like just the two of us, like some kind of couple. If we're gonna go, it should be with the whole group."

"The whole group," Jackson mumbles, so obviously not loving that idea. Snatching a pen off the desk, he fidgets with it, rolling it between his fingers in that agitated way of his.

"Look, I'm sorry. I know that's probably not how you pictured it, but—"

"Why?" He turns to me, his eyes dark with intensity. "Why do you want to break our deal? Do you seriously not want to go with me?"

"I do, I just..." Ugh. I hate this! I don't want to hurt Jackson's feelings.

That look of disappointed confusion is killing me.

"The truth is... I have a boyfriend, and I don't feel right about going with you like we're a couple or something. I mean, I know we'd just be going as friends, but still. It'll be weird, and he doesn't love the idea of me going with just you. I think the friends group will work way better."

Jackson looks like he's just been punched in the gut. "A boyfriend? When? Who?"

I bite my lip and try to figure out how to word things in a way that won't make Jackson's skin turn any paler. "His name's Josh. You don't know him. I met him at a party a few weeks ago. I was out with the girls, and we ended up— You know, it doesn't matter." I cut the story short, doubting Jackson would be impressed that I went to some wild party outside of town. "Anyway, he's a really sweet guy, and I haven't really told anyone about him yet. It's new and we're still finding our way, you know? It's kind of fun having this secret boyfriend. I mean, the truth will come out eventually, but that's why he's not taking me to prom. I just need to figure out a way to tell my parents I'm dating this guy. He's my first boyfriend and…" My voice trails off.

Jackson has slumped back in his seat like I'm lecturing him instead of explaining this wonderful thing that's happening to me.

"Look, I'm sorry, okay? I know we had a deal, but—"

"It's not that," Jackson murmurs.

"Then what is it?"

He blinks, like he only just realized what he said. "Nothing. I…" Snatching his bag, he shoots out of his chair. "Hey, I'm sorry. I gotta… I can't today, I just…" He starts walking away without a backward glance.

I frown at his retreating butt and can't decide how to feel.

He looked so gutted, and I feel kind of guilty about that, but I'm happy, and as my friend, I feel like he should be stoked for me.

I've had to watch him flirt with other girls over the years. Heck, even Simone was after him for a while, and watching those two laughing together nearly killed me. But I didn't complain. I didn't make a fuss.

Not that they ever officially went out or anything.

I just...

Maybe Jackson hasn't gotten over me since he tried to kiss me last year. Maybe he agreed to platonic but never really felt it.

A smile curls my lips, but I wipe it off my face.

I have a boyfriend now.

My phone on the table starts vibrating, and I snatch it up, happy to be distracted by whoever is calling.

A smile stretches my mouth wide as I answer, "Hey, Shay. What's up?"

"Hey, future sister-in-law."

I laugh, loving the sound of that. My older brother, Nate, has been dating Shay since his senior year of high school, and they got engaged at Christmas. It's so exciting. Mom's freaking over the moon, and Dad is stoked too. Everyone is managing to lay their differences aside for the sake of this celebration, and so far, wedding plans are going smoothly.

They're getting married this summer in Portland, where they currently live, and we're all flying from our respective homes to be a part of it. I've been measured up for a bridesmaid dress already, and the only thing I have left to worry about is shoes.

"So, I'm just calling to talk about the reception. Do you have a minute?"

"Yeah, sure."

"There are so many people we want to invite, but my parents can't afford to cater for everyone, so we're thinking we'll have a formal dinner for family and our closest friends, but then invite a bunch of our other friends for dessert and dancing. That way they can hear the speeches and be with us for the party stuff."

"Great idea."

"Yay! Glad you like it. So, now my question is… how would you feel about designing some killer desserts?"

"Oooo." A thrill races through me. "What are you thinking?"

"Well, I'm kind of loving the idea of wedding cupcakes. Do you think that's lame?"

"No! I love it! We could do a bunch of different wedding designs." I sit forward in my seat, snatching a sheet of paper and starting to doodle my thoughts. "We could keep them in your theme colors and do like a series of five or six designs repeated. And the great thing is all of that can be done in advance."

My paper is soon covered with love hearts, tulips (Shay's favorite flower), and then I go a little off course and start thinking about how we could incorporate natural greenery and maybe some cute blueberries for a pop of color.

"I'm doodling a bunch of stuff as we speak."

"You are the best!" Shay's voice pitches with excitement. "Can you send me a photo once you're done, and I'll let you know what I like best?"

"Will do."

Man, I love this! I love that Shay has asked me to be more than just a bridesmaid. My designs will be on display for all her friends. It's thrilling.

"So, have you made up your mind about bringing Jackson yet?"

"Huh?" My pen draws a crooked line down my page.

Shay giggles. "You know. I said you could bring a plus-one if you wanted. I just assumed you'd bring Jackson, because he took you to New York for his brother's wedding."

"Oh, um... I, uh... haven't asked him yet."

There's a long pause, and I know Shay's picked up something in my voice. Dammit! She knows me too well.

"Hailey." She draws out my name, and I tense for whatever she's about to say next. "Is everything okay with you two?"

"Yeah, totally. Why wouldn't it be?" Crap, my voice is too high, my words too fast.

"I don't know, you just sound weird."

"No." I shake my head. "Nothing weird. Just distracted by cupcake designs."

Shay laughs, but I don't think she believes me. Time to cut this call short!

"Hey, I better go. I'll send you a picture soon, okay?"

"Okay. Love you."

"Love you too."

The second I hang up, I drop my pen and let out a shaky breath.

Jackson's forlorn expression whistles through my brain, making me feel like total crap.

Have I just ruined everything with him?

Will he ever talk to me again?

Closing my eyes, I try to remind myself that Josh being my boyfriend is a good thing, but all I can picture is Jackson walking into Joyous Cupcakes. We were eleven years old, and it was the first time we ever saw each other.

I've had a crush ever since.

9

CUPCAKES FOR STARTERS AND DESSERT

THE BELL above the shop door rings as Brody slips into Joyous Cupcakes. The smell hits him first, just like it always does, as a smile stretches across his face. There's no way someone can walk into this place and not feel happy.

"Well, good afternoon, Brody Barrett. How are you?"

"Hey, Joy." He grins at the shop owner. "Just picking up some cupcakes for my lady."

"The same as usual?"

"Probably." He nods, gazing down at the selection. "Unless you've got something new to entice me."

"Well, I've been playing around with a banana caramel swirl. My sister swears it's the best thing I've ever made."

"Mm. Sounds great. I'll take two of those along with the usual order."

"Fantastic." Joy's sunny face beams a little brighter as she gets out a box and carefully starts loading it up with her amazing creations.

Brody pulls out his wallet to pay. "Hailey around today?"

"Not today." Joy shakes her head. "That girl is getting so busy with school. She keeps calling to ask if she can work on different days." Joy rolls her eyes. "She used to live for this place, but her social life has taken off over the last couple years, and this last month has been the worst. Trying to pin her down is nearly impossible."

"Yeah, Jackson's getting busier too, and now that he's got his license..." He trails off with a soft laugh, remembering how little Jackson was when he first met him. He's grown so much, and it seems to have happened overnight.

"Don't I know it. Thankfully, Hailey's been a bit slower with that. She's still on her learner's for a few more months."

"It comes around quick. I can't believe how much of a man Jackson is now. It's kind of scary."

"I know it. Gosh, I can still remember when Hailey was born. She was the cutest baby. And boy, did she have a set of lungs on her." Joy chuckles as she carefully closes the box, making sure not to smear any icing up the sides.

Thoughts of a new baby at the ranch make Brody pause. That's really going to change the dynamics in the house. Crying. Pooping. Michael and Annie will be sleep-deprived.

One of Brody's foster families had a newborn, and all he remembers is bleary-eyed, slightly irritable adults shuffling around the house.

It makes him grateful that he doesn't live at the ranch anymore. He misses it sometimes, but the fact that he gets to work there every day takes the edge off any kind of homesickness.

I wonder when Indy will want to start having a family.

Sliding his card through the machine, he figures it won't be anytime soon. Indy's still in the throws of her vet training. Having worked as a technician for a couple years, she decided to take the plunge and become a large animal vet. It's keeping her busy, and one of the reasons they decided to move closer to town was so she didn't have to commute so far.

Brody doesn't mind having to drive each day. His hours are way more predictable, and he hates the idea of Indy driving after a full, tiring day of either study or work.

Living in Harborton is working really well for both of them.

"Thanks, Joy." He tucks the cupcake box under his arm and heads back to his pickup truck.

For reasons he can't even explain, Brody didn't love the idea of living with Indy and not being married to her, which is why he told her in Vegas that he wanted to get married as soon as they could. She gave him an adoring smile, then surprised them both by suggesting they do it right there and then.

"Are you serious?" Brody's eyes bulged as he gripped her arms and practically lifted her off her feet.

"Well, I mean, yeah. But only if you want to."

"I totally want to."

Her smile started to shine brighter than the casino lights around them. "Let's do it!"

He couldn't be happier that he got married in jeans

and a sweatshirt while Indy stood before him in heels, ripped jeans, and his Adidas hoodie. She'd never looked more beautiful.

Vowing to love and cherish her was the easiest thing in the world, and when she held his hand and said, "I do," with that loving look on her face, he teared up. He couldn't help it.

They didn't bother with rings and instead bought matching necklaces. He fingers the gold disc through the fabric of his T-shirt. Engraved with their names and the day they got married, he's vowed to never take it off. Indy always wears hers too, and every time he sees it resting against her smooth skin, it makes his heart sing.

His wife.

His beautiful wife.

Slipping into the truck, thoughts of Deeks's anger in the barn steal the warm fuzz floating through him. He should have told his brothers sooner. He left it too long, and then it got awkward. But now it's even worse, and he hates the idea of Deeks being mad at him.

Deeks is only pissed off because he's hurt. The others were all surprised but didn't seem too bothered. But maybe they were hurt under the surface as well. It is pretty bad that he kept his marriage a secret. When he reflects on it, he doesn't even know why he did.

Was it just the thrill of the secret?

At the time, it felt kind of romantic, but now it just seems selfish and lame.

Walking in the front door, he spots Indy coming out of their room and holds up the box of cupcakes.

"I knew there was a reason why I married you." She winks at him, giggling when she reaches him, and he holds the box up too high, then pulls her against his side for a thorough kiss.

He waits until she lets out that delicious moan of pleasure before pulling away and passing her the box.

"Ooo! Are there new ones in here?"

"Banana caramel."

"Yum!" She tips her head back, rushing to the table to open the box and taste one.

Watching her lick the icing off her lips makes his insides yearn, and he steps up to the table, running his hand down her back and grabbing out a cupcake of his own.

"So, cupcakes for dinner, then?" He talks with his mouth full.

Indy laughs. "No, I've already chopped up the veggies and chicken for a stir-fry."

"Nice! Cupcakes for starters *and* dessert, then."

"I don't see anything wrong with that." She takes another huge bite, smearing frosting across her cheek.

He laughs and bends down to nip it off her skin. "Mmm. Gimme me a little more of that sugar." He muffles Indy's giggle with his mouth, deepening the kiss and nearly carrying her through to the bedroom.

"Oh no you don't." She stops him. "Last time you took me in there for afternoon delight, I got zero studying done and we forgot to eat dinner. However, if you'd be willing to cook, then I can quickly get some work done and we can go to bed early." She wiggles her eyebrows, and Brody reluctantly places her on her feet.

"Thank you, baby." Her sweet lips brush against his before he steps into the kitchen and gets to work.

Indy loses herself in some online study, her short fingers tapping over the keys with speed. Brody listens to the hurried clicking, taking his time to make sure the brown rice is cooked to perfection before plating it up with the rainbow-colored stir-fry. It smells so freaking good.

"Okay, my love. Time to stop working and start marveling at my culinary skills."

Taking the glass of wine he hands her, Indy moves away from the computer and sits adjacent to him at the table.

"So, baby. How was your day?"

"Yeah, good." Brody launches into a story about the bulls he named Hubert and Harry.

Indy's laughing so hard by the end, she can barely swallow her food.

"Okay, stop. I'll never finish my dinner at this rate." Wiping her mouth with the napkin, she clears her throat and takes a delicate scoop of rice onto her fork. "Talk about something not funny for just a minute. Give me a chance to eat."

Pulling in a breath, Brody holds it for a second, then deflates on a sigh. "I think I really hurt my brothers by not telling them we got married."

"What?" Indy blinks, her lips parting as she gazes across the table.

"I was going to tell you last night, but you were so exhausted after your day that I didn't want to get into it. You needed your sleep, so I just stuck to the happy news about Annie and left out the bad part about our secret."

"So everyone knows?"

"By now they probably will." He points his fork at her. "Expect some phone calls."

"I had my phone off today because I was trying to focus. I bet there are a bunch of messages on there." She goes to grab her purse, then changes her mind with a little head-shake. "I'll deal with it later. How'd they find out?"

"I let it slip yesterday, when we were working in the barn. Deeks was so pissed."

Indy winces. "Oh no. We were afraid that might happen. We shouldn't have left it so long."

"I know." Brody shakes his head, scraping his fork through the pile of rice and scattering grains across his plate. "I feel really bad."

"But we had good reason not to do a big event like Ashlyn and Cooper."

"I think they're more annoyed about the fact that we didn't even tell them. Not inviting them sucked, but not even telling them?"

Rubbing her hand up and down her arm, Indy shoots him a guilty frown. "How can we make it up to them? Maybe we could throw a party to celebrate."

"It's probably too late for that now."

"Well, maybe we just need to sit them all down and give them a sincere apology."

"Yeah." Brody nods, reaching across the table and taking Indy's hand in his.

"It'll be okay. They're family. They'll forgive us."

"Yeah." He tries to match her smile, but his brain is busy figuring out when they can have a family dinner so he can tell them all how sorry he is. He never meant to let them down.

10

HAVING HAILEY'S BACK

I FEEL like I've let Hailey down. I can't even explain why, but I just... She should be going to prom with me, dammit! If I hadn't screwed things up, then she wouldn't be dating some other guy.

Who the hell is Josh, anyway?

She said I wouldn't know him, but this town is freaking small. I can find out what I need to know.

Having spent most of the night tossing and turning in bed, I've got the energy of a sloth as I drive up to school. Thankfully, I also have the determination of a hungry lion. I will not rest until I find out who has stolen Hailey's heart.

He better be good enough for her. That's all I need to know. As much as it will suck, if I find out he's a really great guy, then I'll walk away. I care about Hailey enough to do the right thing.

But not until I know that he's gonna treat her like a freaking queen. That's the least she deserves.

Sweet Hailey.

Beautiful Hailey.

Amazing Hailey.

Why? Why? Why didn't I let her kiss me?

Why did I wait so freaking long to make my move and then let her "friendship" talk scare me off so far?

When she was giving it to me, I could almost sense that she didn't really mean it, but I was too afraid to believe that, and I didn't want to be the idiot who just wouldn't give up.

I thought prom would be my next opening, but I waited too dang long, and now I'm paying for my stupidity.

Pulling into a parking space, I notice one of our friends ambling past. Hailey had said she went to a party and met Josh, so maybe Tash knows something about that. Those girls are pretty tight.

"Tash! Tash!" I call her name before I even cut the engine, jumping out of my truck and chasing after her.

"What is your problem?" She laughs at me stumbling over my feet and dropping my bag in my haste to reach her.

"Sorry," I puff out, collecting my bag off the ground

and throwing it over my shoulder. "Hey, can I talk to you for a sec?"

"Sure." She shrugs.

I lead her away from the crowd of students congregating near the stairs.

"Are you okay?" Her nervous confusion is kind of sweet, and I let her off the hook as soon as we're around the corner.

"Did you know Hailey has a boyfriend?"

She blanches for just a second, then looks to the ground. "I don't know what you're talking about."

"Oh, save it," I whisper. "She told me yesterday."

"She did?" Tash's head pops back up. "When?"

"Uh… I saw her yesterday afternoon." I'm still not sure if Tash knows about our tutoring sessions, so I quickly hedge to cover Hailey's back. "I wanted to talk to her in private so I could ask her to go to prom with me."

"You did? I knew you still had a thing for her." Her voice lights with excitement. "I told Petra we weren't imagining it. Those looks you give her when she doesn't know you're watching." Her expression gets all mushy, and I look away with a disappointed huff.

"We made a deal years ago that we'd go together, but now she doesn't want to because of…"

"Josh."

"Yeah. What do you know about him?"

"Not too much." She shrugs. "Hailey and him kind of stick to themselves when they can be together. I know he's training to be a mechanic."

"At the auto shop in town?"

"I assume so." Tash nods.

"Okay. Okay. So how old is he?"

"Not sure. Nineteen maybe? He didn't look that much older than us."

"Ugh."

Tash giggles. "What's wrong with nineteen?"

"Nothing," I spit, feeling young and pathetic. How the hell am I supposed to compete with a nineteen-year-old mechanic?

Tash's expression crumples with sympathy. "I'm really sorry that things haven't worked out for you and Hailey, but she seems really buzzy and happy with this Josh guy."

Great. That makes me feel even worse.

I mean, it shouldn't. It's great that she's happy. I just want her to be happy with me.

"Do you like him?" I mutter, scuffing the ground with my shoe.

"I've only met him like twice, but he seemed nice enough."

I bob my head, but the edges of my heart are raw and tender. It freaking hurts. I hate this feeling.

"Does he treat her well?"

"I assume so." Tash's lack of conviction makes me frown. She's one of Hailey's best friends. How could she not know? Girls always talk about that kind of stuff, don't they?

"What does that mean?" I ask.

"Look, I don't really know. I don't see them together. And she texts sometimes, all gushy, but... I don't know him, so..."

"Well, does she tell you anything?"

Tash's cheeks flare with color, and she bites her lip.

"What? Tell me. I don't care what it is."

"Are you sure?"

Taking her arms, I gently grip them and lower my head so she's forced to look at my face. "Tell me."

"Okay, fine. All I know is that most afternoons he picks her up and drives her somewhere so they can make out."

"Make out." My throat is suddenly filled with ash. "Somewhere private."

Tash nods.

"Hot and heavy?" Dude, why am I asking this stuff?

"I don't know how hot and heavy, but... I'm guessing it's kind of steamy. Her texts are all like 'Josh is so hot.'"

I swallow, the bitter taste in my throat making it hurt. "Do you think she's sleeping with him?"

"She hasn't told me, so..."

"Would she tell you?"

"I..." She gives a helpless shrug. "I don't know."

"She said they only met like three weeks ago!" My desperation is showing and I can't even stop it.

She gives me a sympathetic smile. "Yeah. Three weeks sounds about right."

"And they're already sleeping together?"

"I don't know if that's happening. I just know they love making out."

I huff, slamming my back against the brick wall and wanting to pound something with my fist. It should be me she's meeting up with after school. The guy who knows her, who cares about her more than anything. I should be the one getting to kiss her.

It's hard to see past the green haze in front of me. I'm probably being a total jerk, but seriously, I hate this.

"Look, I think it's really sweet you're checking the guy out to make sure he's good enough for her." Tash touches my arm, her smile kind. "You've always cared so much about Hailey, and I like that you've got her back. Never stop doing that, no matter who she's with."

Tash pats my arm and then gets distracted by her phone. As she starts texting whoever, I mumble my thanks and slip away, entering the building through the back and shuffling to class.

Her words eat at me.

The whole having Hailey's back thing. Why did she say that? Is she worried about this Josh guy? Is he bad news? Tash didn't seem to know much; not enough for my liking, anyway.

By the time lunch rolls around, I'm freaking obsessed. There's no way I'll be able to concentrate on anything until I at least try to find out more.

Abandoning my buddies before I even reach the cafeteria, I sneak out of school and drive into town. I know where the auto shop is and decide to linger outside the garage to look for some guy who must be around nineteen.

I see one.

He's tall and lanky with a shaved head and a narrow face. He's wiping his hands on a rag and talking to... oh, that's Mr. Whitmore, the guy who owns the garage.

They have a quick chat, and then Josh (it's gotta be him, right?) runs to his car and jumps in. Like some police detective, I start my engine and follow him.

If anyone finds out I'm doing this, there'll no doubt be hell to pay, but I can't help myself. I just need to make sure this Josh guy is okay, and stalking him for one afternoon will tell me enough. If I see him smile and talk nicely to people, maybe help an old lady cross the street or do something kind, then I'm just going to have to accept the fact that Hailey's never gonna be mine.

But if he runs one stop sign, throws gum out his window, or does anything that makes him a jerk, I'm gonna be all over that shit.

Trying to drive like I'm not following him is really challenging. I make sure I put a car between us and try to drive casual so no one will realize just how tense I am. He makes one stop at the grocery store, and I park on the other side of the road, ducking down so no one can see me just sitting there. Crap, if someone notices me, they'll no doubt call the school wondering why I'm playing hooky.

That's one of the most annoying things about living in a small town. Everyone knows everyone, and some people think that gives them the right to make your business their own.

Maybe I should just head back and cut my losses.

But there he is again.

I ping straight, starting my engine as soon as he slips into his car. He takes off, driving farther out of town and stopping on the outskirts, before country roads kick in for real.

Parking behind an abandoned building where high school students are dared to venture after dark, I watch Josh get out of his car. Holding my breath, I ease my truck behind a clump of trees and jump out, sneaking through the foliage until I can see him again.

What's he up to?

His gaze is kind of shifty as he glances over his shoulders, then swaggers up to some guy leaning against the wall.

They grin at each other. I stand taller, watching the exchange from my hiding spot. Neither one of them has noticed me, so that's good. At least I hope they haven't.

Narrowing my eyes, my nostrils flare when I see Josh slip a little baggy out of his pocket. He shakes hands with the guy, doing one of those smooth "only in the movies" kind of exchanges. A second later, he's flicking through a wad of cash before nodding and spinning to leave.

"Holy crap," I whisper. *Did I just watch a drug deal?*

I'm guessing it wasn't white candy he was handing over for a chunk of greenbacks.

This couldn't be more dodgy if I wrote it in a novel.

Josh has nearly reached his car when he glances up and stares right at my hiding spot. I panic and duck down, probably making the foliage shake and move.

Holding my breath, I lie low until I'm certain I hear the sound of an engine accelerating away. Even then, I count to one hundred before checking to make sure the coast is clear.

I can't believe this.

Hailey's dating a drug dealer!

Does she know?

Has he been getting her high at their secret little make-out sessions?

No! Please don't let that be true.

I have to talk to her. I have to tell her what I saw.

She can't date this guy! It's not safe.

Flooring it back to school, I pull into the parking lot, ready to jump out and run to Hailey's class. I'll come up with an excuse. Teachers like me. I'm a good kid. They'll believe whatever I say to them.

But before I can even open my door, Principal Darnell is rapping on my window.

Closing my eyes, I slump back against my seat and let him open the door for me.

"Well, Mr. Wilson. You have some explaining to do, young man. Come with me."

Sliding out of the car, I slam the door behind me, then shuffle after him.

I guess talking to Hailey will have to wait.

Crap. Could this day get any worse?

11

MORE THAN A BLIP

ANNIE RUNS her fingers around the glass of iced tea on the table. Catching the drops of condensation, she licks them off her fingertips and steals a glance at Ashlyn.

The tall, slender woman is sitting on the porch, her legs stretched out in front of her, basking in the sunlight while they enjoy a much-needed break.

It's the little moment of peace they snatch together most afternoons, before the kids get back from school and the men show up, hungry for a snack and with more chores to share around. There's always something to do on the ranch, and Annie loves that. She's never been happier than in this place.

But she's going to have different jobs to do soon, and the idea makes her ill with nerves.

"Stop thinking about it," Ashlyn murmurs. "I've got my eyes closed, but I can tell that's what you're doing. Your poor brain is ticking so hard and fast it's going to implode."

"It's not like I can help it. I'm gonna have a baby. I'm gonna get fat and then have to push the thing out of me."

Ashlyn snickers.

"Don't you laugh."

"Sorry." Ashlyn sits up with a chagrined smile. "I know it's scary, but, Annie, you're gonna be so great."

"I don't know if I've got what it takes to be a mama."

"What are you talking about? You've practically raised Jackson and Arley. You are the mama bear of the Barrett family. I don't understand what you're so worried about."

Annie shakes her head, looking out at the surrounding fields with a frown. "My mom was around for Jackson's baby years." Annie blinks, tears burning her eyes. "I miss her so much right now. I wish she was here."

Reaching out a sympathetic hand, Ashlyn rubs Annie's arm. "I'm sorry she's not. Life is so unfair sometimes."

Annie sniffs, not bothering to wipe away the tear trailing down her cheek.

"I don't know if this will make you feel any better, but you have us. We're your family, and we're going to help you through this. Michael will be such a wonderful father."

"I know that." Annie can't help a smile. Slashing the tears off her face, she sits up and runs a hand over her belly. "He's so sweet and kind. Grandpa Ray would be proud."

"He would."

The women nod, knowing this to be true. Even though they never met the man, they've heard so many stories it's like he still lingers here. His presence can be felt in every room, and the many photos adorning the walls make it feel like he's watching with a smile.

Running her hand over her ring finger, Annie wonders if they'll get married before the baby comes. Michael's sweet words about marrying her because he loved her so dang much just about made her cry. She never thought she'd get this lucky. It helps to still the fears of this impending change, knowing they'll be facing it together.

I wonder when he'll ask me.

Jackson's demand that it better be a good proposal made her grin. She doesn't need anything fancy. She just wants genuine, and she knows she'll get that from Michael Barrett.

"Phone's ringing," Ashlyn murmurs.

"I'll get it." Annie jumps up and heads inside, snatching it off the hook. "Barrett home, Annie speaking."

"Hello, Miss Birdman, it's Principal Darnell from the high school. I'm calling about your brother, Jackson."

Annie grips the phone. The principal's tone is hardly one of warmth, and it sends a shock wave running through her. "Is everything okay?"

"He was caught skipping out of school today. He ended up missing nearly two full periods. I'm sure I don't have to tell you that this is completely unacceptable behavior."

"You most certainly don't!" Annie's surprise makes her voice snappy. She clears her throat, not wanting to yell at the principal. "I can't believe he did that. It's so unlike him, right? I mean, right? Oh gosh, please don't tell me this is a regular thing and you're only just updating me now."

"No. We definitely would have called you. This behavior *is* unlike Jackson, but he's refusing to tell me where he was and why he skipped school."

"Well, I will definitely make him tell me!" Annie huffs, embarrassed that her brother so blatantly broke the rules. "Does the school have some kind of consequences for him?"

"Ah, yes, he'll have to make up the time he missed in detention. If it's okay with you, I'll be keeping him both today and tomorrow."

"Please do. Thank you, sir."

"I'm sure it was just a onetime thing. Thanks for your support, Miss Birdman."

Slamming the phone back down, Annie glares at it for a moment before snatching it back off the hook and dialing her little brother.

"I'm not supposed to answer the phone at school," Jackson skips the pleasantries and gets right to the point. "I've already got detention this afternoon."

"Well, I didn't want you heading off to that before getting an earful from me! What is wrong with you? Playing hooky? Getting caught by the principal?"

"I didn't mean to get caught."

"Jackson!"

"All right, I'm sorry. But I can't change anything now, and you yelling at me isn't helping."

"What were you doin'? Huh? Why'd you skip school?" There's a pause that's too long and ominous for Annie's liking. "Jackson, you better answer me."

"I… There was something I had to do."

"What?"

"I don't want to tell you."

Annie bristles. "Yet you will."

"No. I don't have to."

"Uh, yes, you do."

Jackson scoffs and mumbles, "You're not my mother, so no, I don't."

The words sting every time he pulls them on her, but she steels herself against them and snaps, "I'm the closest thing you've got to one! As your guardian, I think I have a right to know why you're playing hooky!"

"Well, as your little brother, I'm pleading the fifth."

"Jackson, you better—"

"I gotta go before I get busted for talking on my phone."

With a short huff, she grips the receiver. "Fine. Enjoy your detention!"

"Oh, I will!"

Annie growls. "You better be home as soon as you're done, you hear me?"

He doesn't say anything, and she can picture Jackson rolling his eyes and pulling a face.

She wants to shout a little more but instead hangs up before she says something she'll regret. She has a special talent for flying off the handle when she's angry.

"Is everything okay?" Kena steps out of the kitchen with a tentative smile.

"Yeah." Annie slumps against the wall. "My stupid brother decided to play hooky today."

"Really?" Kena's face lights with a grin. "Wow. Jackson? But he's so good."

"Normally. I don't know what the hell has gotten into him."

"It's only one slip up." Kena shrugs. "I wouldn't get too mad over it. Hooky isn't that big of a deal."

Annie humphs. "It depends what he was doing while he was playing hooky."

Kena bobs her head. "Good point."

"School's giving him detention today and tomorrow. Hopefully that'll teach him somethin'."

"Oh, so he's going to be late out of school?" Glancing at her watch, Kena heads for the table. "I guess I better go collect Arley, then. Crap, I'll be late."

"Don't worry about it. I'll call Indy. She and Brody are coming for dinner anyway. I think she's studying from home right now." Annie grabs the phone and makes another call, arranging Indy to get Arley so Kena doesn't have to make the drive and be late.

Once that's done, she slumps down at the dining room table with an exhausted sigh.

"What's up in here?" Ashlyn breezes through the front door while Kena gets Annie a glass of water and rubs her shoulders.

"Jackson played hooky and got detention."

"No way." Ashlyn's eyebrows pop high in surprise. "Jackson?"

"That's what I said." Kena smirks.

"Do you think it's the baby?" Annie looks between them, her blue eyes wide and anxious. "He took the news pretty bad. Do you think he's acting out to punish me or somethin'?"

"No. Of course not." Ashlyn takes a seat beside her. "Jackson is not that immature. He loves you, Annie."

"He's a teenager living in far from normal circumstances," Annie grumbles.

Kena crosses her arms and leans against the table. "But life doesn't have to be normal to work out just fine. He's surrounded by people who love him. Whatever this little blip is will smooth itself out. I wouldn't make a big deal out of it."

"Yeah, I guess." Rubbing her pounding head, Annie takes the water with an unsteady hand and gulps it down.

She can't shake the feeling that Jackson's behavior this afternoon is so much more than a blip.

12

BEST FRIENDS

Jackson

DETENTION WASN'T SO BAD. I just had to sit there and write a one- page essay on the benefits of education. I scribbled down some fluff about the empowerment of knowledge, then spent the rest of the hour doodling Hailey's name in the back of my notebook.

I went from whimsical swirls to bold, dark letters with blue-ink blood dripping off the H and the y.

She has a boyfriend.

A boyfriend who deals drugs.

Shit, I can't believe it.

What am I gonna do?

I have to talk to her, find out if she even knows.

Surely she wouldn't be with this guy if she did.

My mind churns as I drive home, my speed slowing to a crawl when I turn onto the road that leads to the ranch. I nearly divert and take Aunt Nell's driveway instead. I could go talk to her; she'd feed me delicious treats and homemade lemonade while I dished out all my problems. With a friendly pat on the arm, she'd tell me something about God taking care of all his children and not to worry about Hailey. She'd probably tell me I was good and brave for trying to look out for her, and then she might even give me some advice like "tell the sheriff," or "let Mr. Whitmore from the auto shop know."

But can I really do that without talking to Hailey first?

I'm guessing Aunt Nell would agree with me. She'd probably give me a hug and tell me to seek out Hailey, knowing just how much I care about her. Then she'd feed me more cookies and assure me that I'm a great kid.

I doubt Annie will have the same reaction.

No, my sister… my guardian… is gonna yell at me the second I walk through the door. I'm so not in the mood for one of her fire blasts, so when I turn into the driveway, I bypass the house and drive all the way down to the barn.

I'm home, aren't I? She can't yell at me for not doing what she told me to.

Michael's in there, putting the finishing touches on the stalls for the new calves. Man, things are about to get busy. As soon as those baby cows come popping out, Arley and I will be on feeding duty. Early mornings and constantly smelling like that gross milk the calves drink is going to be a big part of my near future. I usually love it. Those calves are cute.

But I'm just not in the mood today.

Not for any of it.

Stomping over the dry hay, I grab a pair of gloves and wriggle them onto my fingers before walking up to Michael and silently getting to work beside him.

"You okay?" Michael asks, his voice just a soft murmur.

I grunt and refuse to look at him.

"Did you skip out on school today?"

I roll my eyes. *Great. Two lectures in one afternoon.* I thought Michael would be the safer option. He's good at not talking. He understands the beauty of silence.

Keeping my lips clamped together, I focus on the work, relieved when he finally murmurs, "Don't worry about it. I'm sure you had good reason."

I pause and turn to him. "I did."

"Want to talk about it?"

"Not really." How do I even start? I don't want to shine Hailey in a bad light. I need to find out what she knows before saying a word to anyone.

He gives me a long, patient look before softly asking, "You didn't do anything illegal though, right?"

"No. Of course not."

"Thought so." The side of Michael's mouth tips up, and he gives me a little wink before turning back to work.

The relief pumping through me is palpable. For a second, I nearly tell him, but he starts talking before I can.

"I'm doing it tonight."

"Huh?"

"The proposal. Everyone will be here for dinner, and I've arranged for Jake and Carmen to call so they can see it too."

"Tonight?" I nod, trying to wrap my brain around this. It's a good thing. A really good thing. Michael's a great guy, and I want my sister to be happy.

Plus, it'll take the spotlight off me and definitely put Annie in a better mood. That's a huge relief.

I guess I just have to be okay with the fact that things are changing. That I'm getting muscled out of this family by a new baby, and my sister is becoming a Barrett.

Like officially.

That peaceful sense of relief starts to fizzle and disappear.

Annie will share Michael's last name, and the jealousy ripping through me is fierce.

"That's okay, right?" Michael's staring at me, worry pinching his eyebrows together.

"Yeah, of course."

"I mean, it won't be anything grand, but I figure it's more important to be authentic. I'm not a grand gesture kind of guy, and when I think about Annie and what matters to her the most, it's family. Proposing to her in front of everyone will make her happy, I think." His lips twitch with a nervous grin.

It's hard not to love this guy. I nod. "Yeah, it'll make her super happy."

His smile grows a little wider. "Thanks, man. Just wanted to give you a heads-up."

"Got a ring?"

"Yeah. I went into town and bought it today." His hands are shaking as he opens a small velvet box. "Kena helped me."

I gaze down at the diamond ring. It's simple. A small, square-shaped diamond sitting on a gold band. I picture Annie's face when she sees it. She's going to be so damn happy. I grin.

Michael closes the box with a soft chuckle. "I'm nervous, man. I'm not great with public speeches, you know?"

"You're gonna be awesome. Just speak from your heart and don't worry about it." I pat his back, and we get back to work.

Less than an hour later, we're driving up to the house, and I stand through a lecture from Annie, yet again refusing to tell her what I was doing but promising it wasn't anything illegal or bad.

"Why won't you just tell me?"

"Because... it's... private."

Her eyes narrow, and she studies me with folded arms. After a frustrated sigh, she shakes her head. "Okay, fine, but will you *promise* me that if you need help or are in any kind of trouble, you'll let me know?"

"I'm not in trouble," I reassure her. "I'm just... trying to protect a friend."

That little bit of truth seems to appease her, and she waves her hand toward the stairs. "Go shower up before dinner."

"Yes, ma'am." She hates when I call her that, and I

throw in a wink and grin to try to snap the tension between us.

It seems to work, and she fights a smile as I run up the stairs.

Well, that went better than I thought. She was less angry than I was expecting her to be, but just in case she gets riled up while I'm upstairs, I take my sweet time showering and getting dressed for dinner. I even stay in my room and get started on homework, not venturing down the stairs until Brody starts booming for everyone to come to the table.

The smells wafting upstairs are freaking mouthwatering. Michael's obviously worked his magic in the kitchen and cooked all of Annie's favorites. The table is a colorful array of dishes, and Annie is gushing over how talented her man is.

We haven't even sat down for grace when Jake and Carmen call in. Michael's face flushes with surprise while Deeks answers and tells them, "You'll have to watch us eat. Dinner's just been served."

"Oh sorry. We had to call early because we're due somewhere in twenty minutes," Jake explains.

"Why are you even calling? Is everything okay?" Annie asks, her hand resting on the back of her chair as she waits to sit down.

I steal a glance at Michael, whose eyes are now bulging, but then he sucks in a breath and grabs Annie's attention.

"Annie, love of my life." He takes her hand, and Brody starts grinning like a fool.

Deeks purses his lips and spins the phone around so Jake and Carmen can see.

Dropping to one knee, Michael pulls out the ring box and holds it up, while Annie covers her mouth, fighting tears.

"You are the best thing that's ever happened to me. You're my sunlight. You make every day brighter and better. I love your strength, your tenacity, your generosity and your beautiful heart. You're my best friend, and I'd love nothing better than to spend the rest of my life with you."

His best friend.

My thoughts run to Hailey. I know I should be in this moment with my sister, but all I can think of is *my* best friend, the girl who I've cared so much about since we started going to school together. I've been lucky to have her in my life for over five years, and I don't want to lose her.

But more than that, I don't want to see her get hurt.

I have to talk to her. I have to tell her about her douche bag boyfriend.

"So, Annie Mae Birdman, will you marry me?"

"Yes." She doesn't even wait a beat. "Yes. A thousand times yes."

Michael's wearing a dopey grin as he slips the ring onto her finger, then stands and pulls her into a hug.

They kiss while everyone around the table cheers. I clap along with them, noticing how Kena's got tears in her eyes. Deeks gives her a worried frown until she glances at him, and he forces a smile. Not sure what that's about, but I dart my attention to Indy and Brody, who are hugging and watching Annie admire her ring with gooey smiles on their faces. Ashlyn and Cooper are next to them, holding hands and sharing a look. They do that a lot, like they're telepathic or something. It's a special thing between them, and it makes me realize how much I want a special thing too.

And there's only one girl I really want it with.

13

AN EARLY MORNING ARGUMENT

Hailey

I STEP out my front door, expecting to walk to Petra's house so she can give me a ride to school. Instead, I find Jackson waiting for me at the base of the steps.

"Hey." He raises his hand, his smile kind of cautious.

I pause on the porch and gaze down at him, my heart expanding like it always does when I study his handsome face.

I wish it wouldn't.

I wish he hadn't gotten better-looking with time.

Puberty did the world some huge favors when it comes to Jackson Wilson. He's grown taller, muscular, his biceps and forearms rippling when he moves. I love watching them, especially when he's controlling a horse or working on the ranch. It's impossible not to stare.

And then there's his face, which is getting stronger and more defined. His jawline is scrumptious, and the amount of times I've imagined my lips skimming along that edge... His light stubble that he never lets grow too long, would tickle my lips and—

Hailey, you're staring! Stop it! You have a boyfriend, remember?

I blink and stutter, "What are you... um, what are you doing here?"

Jackson spins the keys around his finger, catching them in his hand. "Can I drive you to school?"

The serious look on his face makes me nervous. I'm still unsettled by our conversation yesterday, but I can't refuse him. With a simple nod, I walk down the stairs and follow him to his car.

He opens the door for me, and as I slip into the passenger seat, my nerves stretch a little tighter.

What's he up to?

Jackson pulls away from the curb and leaves me in silent suspense until I can barely take it. I text Petra to let her know I've got a ride to school, then tap my thumb on my phone screen, waiting for him to talk.

What's taking him so long?

Why did he want to drive me to school?

What's going on?

I'm about to blurt out a bunch of questions when he clears his throat.

I glance at him, raising my eyebrows. He throws me a

quick look before turning back to the road and murmuring, "So, I've gotta tell you something, but it's way awkward, and I don't know how to begin."

"Okay." I nod. "Well, it's me, you know? You can tell me anything."

"Yeah." He tips his head, and his expression says he doesn't believe me. "I guess it's kind of different now, though."

"Why?"

"Because you have a boyfriend."

I sigh and cringe. "Just because I have a boyfriend doesn't mean we can't still be friends."

As soon as the words pop out of my mouth, I can feel how wrong and false they sound.

Why?

Because Jackson's always been the friend I've crushed on, the one who could potentially turn into something more. And I must be that for him too, right? His reaction yesterday and this conversation right now are making that abundantly clear.

I shift in my seat, keeping my eyes on the road ahead and feeling a nervous heat rise through me.

Crap! This is bad! Am I seriously losing Jackson?

The thought makes me want to cry, but then he starts talking again and I'm distracted from tears.

"Okay, so we're friends. And friends look out for each other, right?"

"Yeah." I answer slowly, this weird sense of caution swirling through me. I notice Jackson tapping his finger on the steering wheel, a sure sign of nerves. "What are you getting at?"

He sighs, then clenches his jaw. Aw man, I'm not going to like whatever he's about to say to me.

I nearly tell him to shut up before he even opens his mouth, but then I'll just spend my day wondering what he wanted to say. It's probably best to just get this over with.

Biting my lips together, I grip my phone and prepare.

"I know something about Josh. Something... very not cool."

I frown. "What? And how? You've never even met the guy."

Scratching the back of his neck, he refuses to look at me, but I turn to face him fully so I can study his profile... and maybe glare at him a little. Why is he trying to ruin what I have with Josh? My first real boyfriend and Jackson's throwing a hissy. Anger is already starting to bubble.

"I drove to the auto shop yesterday. I wanted to know what he looked like, and I ended up following him."

And the anger explodes. "You stalked my boyfriend?"

"I just wanted to get a read on the guy."

"Why? You don't trust my judgment? Do you have any idea how insulting that is?"

He glances at me, then back to the road. "I just want you to be safe."

"And why wouldn't Josh be safe?"

Clamping his lips together, I watch the muscle in his jaw work, then end up thumping back in my seat.

"Argh!" I cross my arms. "I can't believe you did that!

It's so over the line… and rude… and who the hell do you think you are to—"

"He's dealing drugs, Hailey!"

Jackson shout shuts me up for a second. My eyes bulge and I shake my head, wondering if I heard him correctly. "What? Don't be insane!"

"I saw him. He gave this guy a little bag of white stuff and then accepted a fat wad of cash in return."

"And how do you know they were drugs? Did you see them?"

"I wasn't close enough to get a good look, but it was so obviously something illegal. They were meeting behind an abandoned building, and it was so freaking sketchy."

"So you sat there like some spy watching it all play out? Why weren't you in school?"

"Seriously?" Jackson balks. "Hailey, I just told you that your boyfriend is selling drugs and you're worried about me skipping school?"

I let out a groan of disgust, slapping my hand on the seat. "I can't believe you did that! How do you even know it was Josh? You've never met him before!"

"Is he a tall grease monkey with a shaved head and—"

"Okay, shut up," I snap, not wanting to hear this.

Josh doesn't deal drugs. He's not like that.

I grit my teeth, glaring out the window and trying to ignore the buzzing in my head.

How do you know he's not like that?

You've only been dating three weeks, and you've basically spent the whole time making out. It's not like you sit there talking about life histories. He doesn't even know your parents are divorced or that you have two older brothers who live out of state. He barely knows anything about you, and you barely know anything about him.

I squeeze my eyes shut, wishing my brain had an off switch. I don't want to hear this stuff! I don't want to know!

I just want to have a nice boyfriend who is a great kisser and likes me.

"I can't believe you did that!" I spit out yet again. "You had no right, Jackson!"

"I'm sorry, okay? But I had to make sure you were safe."

"Stop talking like that!" I swivel back to face him. I feel like my cheeks are on fire—hot with rage and indignation. "I'm not your responsibility. Stop treating me like some kid that you need to keep an eye on."

"You're my best friend!" He looks at me, his face the picture of hurt and annoyance. "Of course I want to look after you."

"Best friends don't go behind each other's back."

"No, they just get secret boyfriends, right?" Jackson's anger flares, the heat in his truck igniting to an inferno.

"I didn't do anything wrong! You don't have to know every detail of my life."

He grunts, his knuckles turning white as he grips the wheel like he wants to snap it off.

"You had your chance! I freaking threw myself at you, and you didn't want me. You can't now turn around and start acting like some jealous freak."

"Had my chance?" He throws me an incredulous look.

"We were twelve, and you tried to kiss me. I'd never kissed anyone before, and I didn't know what to do. Excuse me for being nervous about it!"

I wish I had some decent comeback, but I can't think of anything to say.

He was nervous? That's so endearing. Dammit!

"And it's not like I didn't try later. It took me years to work up the courage to act on my feelings, and when I finally did, *you* weren't interested!"

"I was scared, okay?" My voice pitches. "I didn't want to get my heart broken again. You have no idea how much your rejection hurt me, and then we stopped talking for a month and it felt like an eternity. I didn't want to do anything to screw up our friendship!"

Jackson winces like that news physically hurts him.

My chest is aching so hard I have to turn away. I glare out the window, my eyeballs burning. But I will *not* cry.

"I'm sorry." Jackson's voice comes out rough and rusty. "I never meant to break your heart. Of course I'd never hurt you on purpose."

I swallow, not wanting to be so damn affected by his sweet words. With a little sniff, I steel myself and challenge him. "Then why did you go behind my back about Josh? If you don't want to hurt me, why make up these lies and try to sabotage my first real relationship?"

"Lies? Sabotage?" He pulls into the school, slamming on the brakes and making us jerk forward when he stops in the parking space. "Do you really think so little of me? I'm trying to protect you."

"That's not your job." I push the door open, my eyes

starting to sting even more. They're going to flood soon, and like hell I'll let Jackson see that. I sprint away from his stupid truck and into school.

I hate arguing with anyone, but arguing with Jackson is a killer.

He wants to protect me. He so obviously cares about me.

But stalking Josh?

That's so wrong!

Slamming into the bathroom, I lock myself in a stall and bury my face in my hands, finally letting the tears fall. I can't believe Jackson did that.

I can't believe Josh might be dealing drugs.

The thoughts sit ugly and cold inside me, and it only makes me cry that much harder.

14

WHAT'S BEST FOR ME

THE REST of my day is a complete suck-fest. I can't face Hailey again, so I spend my lunchtime in the library and then have to suffer a Friday afternoon detention before I can be free.

I broke Hailey's heart.

Yeah, it was years ago, but I hurt her enough that she didn't want to risk anything with me again.

I feel like total crap.

The idea of her being upset with me is the worst, and I don't know what to do with myself. Maybe crawl into a cave and disappear for a few years. That sounds pretty perfect to me.

Jerking to a stop outside the house, I grab my backpack and head inside. I don't know what I'm going to find today. Will Annie still be pissed enough to lecture me again? Will Michael have a load of chores to get through before dinner?

I ease open the back door and am surprised by how quiet everything is.

Slipping off my shoes, I line them up next to the others and pad through the kitchen. I think the house is empty until I spot my sister on the couch, gazing at her engagement ring with a dreamy smile.

Ugh.

Please don't talk wedding plans. Please don't drag me into a conversation about love and all that bullshit.

Annie's head pops up, and she beams me a smile. "Hey."

"Hi." I shuffle on my feet, gripping my bag strap and trying to come up with an excuse to bail.

"Jack Jack!" Arley runs into the room, saving my butt and making me grin as she launches herself into my arms.

"Wanna go for a walk, kiddo?"

"Yes!"

I place her on her feet.

"Can you guys go up to Ashlyn's for me?" Annie gets up off the couch, swaying for just a moment and touching her forehead.

"Are you okay?" I jerk toward her.

"Yeah, I'm fine." She waves me off. "Apparently pregnancy makes you a little light-headed sometimes. The doctor gave me the rundown. I've got so much to look forward to." She gives me a sarcastic smile before laughing and walking through to the office. "Ashlyn asked to borrow this book. I just finished it this afternoon."

I take it out of her hand and skim the cover. Looks like some girly historical fiction. I nod, swallowing back my sarcastic quip and forcing a smile instead.

"Okay, kiddo," I say to Arley. "Let's get our shoes on."

Arley runs into the kitchen and I trail behind her, glad the weather outside is so warm and sunny. A walk up to Cooper and Ashlyn's place will be just what I need to kill this restless feeling.

At least I hope it will be.

Arley skips ahead of me up the pathway. I squint my eyes against the sun, wishing I'd remembered to grab my shades. Pulling my baseball cap a little lower, I shade my face, studying the fields around us.

Man, this place is awesome.

When we reach the top of the rise, we spot Ashlyn in the field next to the house, brushing down her horse. She has a contented smile on her face and is humming a tune. I grab Arley's hand and slow our approach. I can see the pods in Ashlyn's ears, and I don't want to scare her.

Arley wriggles free of my grasp and runs for the chicken coop.

"Hey, chickadees!" she chirps, crouching down by the mesh and chatting away like she always does.

Ashlyn must have caught the movement out of the corner of her eye, because she spins around, pulling out her ear pods and grinning. "Hey, you guys."

"Hey." I hold the book up. "Annie asked me to deliver this."

"Oh great." She drops the brush at her mare's feet and wanders over to the fence. "Fantastic. I've been wanting to read this ever since Kena told me about it. Apparently it's an amazing book."

I nod, not wanting to tell her that I think it looks incredibly boring.

She runs her thumb over the pages and then looks at me, the smile slipping from her face. "You okay?"

"Uh-huh." I nod, shoving my hands in my pockets.

Ashlyn snickers and shakes her head. "No you're not. Want to talk about it?"

"Not really."

Her snicker turns to a giggle. "Just like your brother. Cooper's not much of a talker either." Her nose wrinkles. "But he always appreciates it after I've made him open up to me."

I shake my head, muttering, "He's not my brother."

Ashlyn doesn't respond immediately. I steal a quick glance and feel like she's stripping me bare with those green eyes of hers. When she finally speaks, her voice is soft. "He basically is."

"Yeah. I guess so." I shrug, wishing I hadn't made that stupid comment.

"Do you not want to be part of the family?"

"Of course I do!" My eyes bulge as I try to backpedal and make this right. "I just... I'm not a Barrett. That's what I meant. Technically, we're not related. My last name's Wilson, and it always will be."

She tips her head to the side, and I watch her long ponytail tumble over her shoulder, curls splaying across her tanned skin. "You know, Cooper's last name is officially Adams, same as Michael, Deeks, Jake, and Brody. But you never hear them calling each other that." Ashlyn smiles at me. "Sometimes we have to pick our own paths, you know. Decide what's best for you and go for it. If you want to be a Barrett, you be one."

Her sweet words and smile make my lips curl up at the corners.

I guess she's kind of right.

It does make me wonder why they all cling so fiercely to the Barrett name. Is it just their love for Grandpa Ray, or is there something more to it?

As I take Arley's hand and we walk back to the house, I can't get the conversation out of my head.

Ashlyn's words about picking paths stay with me. I have to decide what's best for me.

Hailey. Hailey is what's best for me, and I screwed it up yet again. I can't keep doing that.

"Hey, Jackson?"

I glance down at Arley. "Yeah?"

"Where are we going for our date tomorrow?"

"Oh, um… I'm still deciding." Crap! I totally forgot about our monthly date. The first or second Saturday of every month, I take her out. Usually for ice cream or a horse ride or something in town. Just a bit of fun for her and me. I started the tradition as soon as I got my license, so it hasn't been going for very long, but Arley will never let me forget about it.

"Can it be somewhere outside in the sun? It's such a nice day, and I love that blue sky!" She smiles up at it, and I can't help adoring her.

"Of course. I just have something to do in the morning first. Then I'll come back and get you, and we'll go on an adventure. Hey, maybe we could do a picnic or something."

"Yay! I love that idea!" She lets go of my hand and starts running down the hill. "I'm gonna tell Dee Dee and Kena!"

As I watch her race off, I can't help being slightly in awe. She's so damn happy. That little girl is an orphan like me. She never gets to call anyone Mom or Dad, but it doesn't seem to bother her. I guess Deeks and Kena are kind of like her parents, but so are Annie and Michael. And I've seen her run to Brody for help, and she loves story time with Ashlyn. This unusual living situation doesn't bother her in the slightest. Man, I hope she stays that way. Who the hell needs normal, right?

Burying my hands in my pockets, I wander back to the house, my brain buzzing with plans for tomorrow.

A picnic with Arley will be fun, but before I can enjoy that, I *have* to make things right with Hailey, and I don't want to do that over the phone.

Whether she wants me to or not, I'm showing up at her house in the morning, and I will apologize until she forgives me. Then I don't know what I'm gonna do. I should probably tell her how much I still care about her, that I possibly even love her.

But she has a boyfriend.

It's complicated.

All I do know is that I can't lose her as a friend. Whether I'm right or wrong about Josh, I need to be there for her. No matter what.

15

BABY TALK

ASHLYN WATCHES Arley and Jackson until they've disappeared from sight.

They are the sweetest.

A maternal instinct she didn't even realized she possessed stirs within her. Watching Jackson grow up over the years has been like watching her own child blossom into a man. But Jackson's not her son. He's not anyone's son, and Ashlyn can't help wondering if that is bothering him more than he's willing to let on.

Rubbing a hand over her heart, she goes back to brushing down Lady and rehashing her conversation with Jackson. When he started lamenting the fact that he wasn't Cooper's brother and had the last name Wilson, Ashlyn had to resist the urge to wrap him in a hug.

"But you're ours," she wanted to say.

I wonder if Annie's pregnancy is making him feel displaced.

She pauses, fingering Lady's mane and thinking that

one through. Should she tell Annie? Probably not; she's stressed enough as it is.

Holding the thought to herself, Ashlyn finishes up her job and ambles back to the house, saying hello to the chickens before stepping onto the porch.

She'll just have to make sure that Jackson knows how much they all love him and what an important part of the family he is. New babies are not going to change that.

"Babies," she whispers to herself. Slipping off her boots, Ashlyn can't help the fleeting idea of getting pregnant too. How fun would it be to experience that at the same time as Annie.

They've become like sisters. They love spending time together, and raising babies together would be the ultimate. They could help and support each other, lament the hard times, celebrate the good times. Figure out their parenting challenges together.

And their kids would be close in age, going to school around the same time, becoming best friends. They would be cousins! It's kind of perfect.

"I love it." Ashlyn giggles to herself, placing the book down on the coffee table and then twirling into the kitchen.

She's just starting dinner prep when Cooper walks in.

"Hey, handsome!" she calls, wondering when to ask him.

Now? She kind of wants to do it right this second, but Cooper's the kind who needs to adapt to big changes more slowly. First you hint, just the most subtle comment to get the brain ticking, then go into more depth a bit later, once he's had time to subconsciously mull. Little conversations here and there help to bring those thoughts to the front of his brain, and soon enough he's making decisions without even knowing how much prep work went into it.

Ashlyn decides to talk about something else first and ease her way into the idea of starting a family.

"Good afternoon, beautiful." Cooper's arms curl around her waist as he nuzzles the back of her neck. Tingles run down her body, igniting embers that can never be fully extinguished, not with Cooper around.

Spinning to face him, she runs her fingers through his hair while he picks her up off the floor and she wraps her legs around him. His grin and that look in his eyes make her skin sizzle. She loves how much he adores her. How he can always make her feel so beautiful without having to say a single word.

She kisses him, taking her time to linger over his mouth and sink into the luxury of his tongue.

His satisfied moan and the way he grips her waist almost makes her forget time, but then the phone in his back pocket dings and they're forced apart.

He checks the text and quickly responds.

"Who was that?"

"Just Michael. It's a work thing that can be dealt with in the morning."

"Cool." Ashlyn turns back to chopping vegetables, popping a piece of carrot in her mouth and munching while she works. "Hey, did you see Jackson on your way up?"

"Nope. Why?"

"I don't know." She shrugs, trying to go for casual. Cooper can worry about stuff and she doesn't want to burden him. "He just said something weird this afternoon, and I guess I'm worried about him."

"What'd he say?"

"That he wasn't your brother."

Cooper's eyebrows pop up in surprise. He takes the carrot piece she feeds him and crunches through it. "I guess technically he's not."

"But he basically is. In all the ways that count."

"True."

"I just worry that he doesn't *feel* like he is. This whole pregnancy and new engagement. I wonder if it's messing with him more than we think. Like he's got it in his head that he doesn't belong or something stupid."

"He belongs. We just have to make sure he knows that loud and clear."

Oh how she loves this man.

Pecking his lips in thanks, she smiles and asks, "Do you think you could have a word with him tomorrow?"

"Me? Wouldn't it be better coming from Michael? He's the closest thing to a father for him."

"I'm just wondering if it'll mean more coming from someone who doesn't *have* to say it to him, you know what I mean?"

Cooper's nose wrinkles in his standard look of reluctance. "Yeah, I guess so. Um... yeah, okay. I suppose I'll make some time to chat with him tomorrow."

"Thanks." Ashlyn kisses him again, the love bubbles

rising in her making it impossible to hide her feelings. Without warning, her eyes start to glisten, the image of her holding a baby that's half her, half Cooper making her want to burst into floods of happy tears.

His calloused hand touches her neck, his eyes deep with concern. "What is it?"

Oh screw the slow buildup. I just want to tell him now!

"Do you want to have kids one day?"

He pauses, jerking with surprise, then blinking a few times. "Annie's pregnancy messing with you too, huh?"

She giggles. "No. It's just got me thinking. For some reason, we've never really talked about kids, and I suddenly realized that's probably irresponsible. I should have asked you if you wanted them before we got married."

She should have, but it wouldn't have been a deal breaker. She and Cooper were destined to be together. She's always wanted him more than anything else.

Cooper crosses his arms and leans against the kitchen counter. "Well, do you want them?"

"Only if they're yours." She gives him a seductive smile.

He grins, the wolfish look in his eyes making her heart tingle. "When do you want to start trying?"

Dropping the knife on the chopping board, she forces his arms apart and steps up against him. "Really? You want to have babies with me?"

He takes his time answering, which is a good thing. This is way too big of a question to be flippant with.

Eventually he starts nodding, his voice husky and

sincere. "I've thought about it before, and I know having a family with you would make me a very happy man."

"Aw, baby. I love you so much." She kisses him and it deepens within moments, fingers gripping clothing as heat rises to a quick, sizzling inferno.

Pulling back, Cooper puffs against her lips, "Seriously. When do you want to start trying?"

She grins. "How about right now?"

With a sexy growl, Cooper lifts her into his arms, carrying her to their bedroom.

Dinner can wait.

Everything can wait.

It's time to make a baby.

16

A PROMISE I DON'T WANT TO MAKE

JOSH'S TONGUE feels heavier than normal.

I know that's a weird thing to think, but it's like he's trying to taste-test my tonsils this afternoon, and I don't like it.

I ease back, not wanting to offend him but also wanting to keep the kissing going. At least I think I do.

His hands glide up my back, pressing me closer against him. I like that feeling. I mean, I love it. Even more so when I'm not rehashing a fight with my best friend.

Dammit!

I try to focus on the moment. I'm sitting on the hood of Josh's car while he stands in front of me, his hand exploring the shape of my back and diving into my hair. He groans and runs his other hand around the curve of my butt, giving it a light squeeze. I can sense his need for me. I get it—some days my body wants the same thing—but I'm still not ready to go all the way, and I definitely can't today. Not with all this Jackson drama swirling around in my head.

"Oh, babe, you feel so good." Josh pants out the words between kisses. "I've never met anyone like you."

He trails his lips along my jaw and starts kissing my neck, his hands wandering up my body. He's getting handsy again. Do I let him? How far will it go today? How long will I let him explore before hitting my limit and quietly pushing him back?

How long will he not mind me doing that?

I shift, angling my body away when he tries to wriggle his fingers under my shirt.

"Come on, don't tease me." He grins, sucking my neck and finding an opening in the back of my shirt. "Let me touch that smooth skin of yours. I love it."

His words are sweet, but still I tense, closing my eyes and trying to force thoughts of Jackson aside.

But I can't!

He wouldn't be touching me like this, not without asking first. He'd stop and check, look me in the eye to make sure I was cool with all of this. I know he would.

Josh starts fiddling with the clasp of my bra, and I lurch back.

"Wait. Slow down."

Pushing on his chest, I get his standard tut of disappointment, but he pulls his hand out from under my shirt and steps back, raising them both in surrender.

"Fine. You're nervous. Whatever. Just please let me know when you're ready, okay?" Placing his hands on either side of my face, he tips my head to look up at him. "I want you, Hailey. Don't make me wait too long."

He smiles like he cares about me, but all I can think is *What if I'm never ready to go all the way with him?*

How will he react then?

Brushing his thumb across my cheekbone, he leans in and starts kissing me again, pushing my lips apart with his tongue.

I like his lips. His hands. I like having a boyfriend.

Making out is fun, but this afternoon it just feels like pressure.

Jackson said he saw Josh dealing drugs.

That one thought is ruining this for me, and I know I won't be able to do anything unless I deal with this.

If Josh is my boyfriend, then I should be able to ask him, right?

Josh pulls away from me, a slight frown pulling his eyebrows together. "Are you all right?"

I blink, not sure what to say.

"It's like you're somewhere else this afternoon. Your kissing is kinda off, and you keep pulling away. Do you not want me anymore?"

"Of course I do." I blush, wondering if he can sense my lie.

Wait. What? My lie?

His eyes narrow as he studies my face.

There's no lie. You still want him, right?

I guess that kind of depends on how this next conversation goes.

I sigh and shuffle back to create some space between us. We need to talk.

"I'm sorry," I murmur. "I guess I am distracted. I got into a fight with one of my friends today, and it's weighing on me."

"Bummer." Josh leans against the car beside me, crossing his arms and ankles.

He's so long and lean. I gaze down at his legs and wonder how much to say.

I should tell him. If I trust this guy and I don't believe what Jackson saw, then I should just be able to ask him.

No big deal, right?

"So, um…" I scratch the side of my nose. "The argument was kind of about you."

"What? Me?" Josh jerks up and stands in front of me. "Why were you talking about me? I thought you and I were a secret."

"We are. I mean, sort of. I kind of had to tell my friend why I wasn't going to prom with him, and then you came up in conversation."

His dark eyebrows dip into a sharp V. "You didn't need to do that. You could have hedged or lied."

"I…" My head jerks back in surprise. "I never lie to Jackson."

"Jackson." He spits the word like it's an unpleasant taste in his mouth. "What is up with him anyway? Why were you arguing about me?"

"Well, he…" I sigh again, my voice turning small and mouse-like. "He thought he saw you…" I bite the tip of my tongue between my lips, then just blurt it. "He saw you selling drugs to someone."

"What?"

I dare to look at his face and don't miss the tight set of his jaw.

"What the hell does he think he's doing, making up lies about me?"

I wince. "That's what I said, but I've been thinking about it all day, and Jackson doesn't lie. And he's not the kind of guy who would try to ruin our relationship. He's… he's just not like that."

"Oh yeah, and how do you know he's not trying to screw up what we've got going out of jealousy or something?"

I dip my head, hating that thought. Would Jackson really stoop so low?

With a sad sigh, I shake my head and look back up at my boyfriend. Lightly fisting the fabric of his overalls, I murmur, "Just tell me that what he saw was a mistake and we can let this go."

"I oughta pound that guy for being such a jerk."

"Please don't." My voice pitches. The idea of Josh hurting my best friend makes my insides writhe. "Let's not make a big deal out of this. What were you doing yesterday afternoon that made him think you were selling drugs? He must have seen it wrong."

Josh shakes his head, his nostrils flaring as he stares out at the water.

"Josh?"

"Of course I wasn't selling drugs," he spits.

He's lying.

The thought is acidic and nasty, making my stomach tense. I squeeze my eyes shut and shake my head, trying to rid myself of the idea. Of course he's not lying.

"You tell your *friend* he better watch his back. Spreading rumors about me will get him into serious trouble."

I don't say anything. I can't. My lips and tongue have stopped working. All I can do is stare at Josh, trying to figure out the truth.

"What?" he snaps. "I don't sell drugs!"

And there it is again. The lie.

How can I tell?

I don't know, it's just a feeling. Or maybe it's the way he can't quite look at me, or the fact that he starts scratching his chest whenever the word "drugs" is mentioned.

"What?" He bulges his eyes, like he's daring me to challenge him.

Okay, fine. I will.

Keeping my voice soft, I say, "I don't know if I believe you."

He scoffs and steps away from the car, his shoes scuffing up the dirt.

"Don't push me, Hailey," he mutters. "I can't have you going around telling everyone I sell drugs. I'm new in town, and it will destroy me."

I frown. "What were you doing yesterday afternoon?"

"Nothing! Working!"

"So, if I go ask your boss, he'll tell me you were at the garage all afternoon?"

His eyes flare with anger, and for a second, I can't deny that snap of fear.

I'm in an isolated spot by the lake with this person I don't really know.

This liar.

Huffing out a breath, he points at me. "Why would you do that, Hailey? Huh? Why won't you believe your boyfriend?" He slaps his chest. "But no, you're willing to swallow down your stupid friend's lie about me!"

"He's not stupid. And I've known him for nearly half my life. He's my best friend."

"He's an idiot."

The insult hurts. And pisses me off.

"At least he doesn't sell drugs," I mutter under my breath.

"That's it." Josh snatches my arm, jerking me off the car and shaking me hard. "Stop staying that shit!"

"Let me go." I try to slap his hand off me, but he just pinches harder.

"No! Not until you promise to keep your mouth shut." His warning glare falters when he obviously realizes what he just said.

I shake my head, unable to hide my scorn. "So, it's true, then."

With a sharp growl, he lashes out, slapping me across the face.

Shock makes me gasp, then blink, as I try to get my head around what the hell just happened.

He slapped me.

The sting is still firing across my face when I launch right back, cracking him across the cheek.

"Don't touch me!" I shout, wrenching my arm out of his grasp and running behind his car.

His long strides quickly catch up to me and he yanks my sleeve, spinning me around and firing his fist into my stomach. I fold in half, shock and pain rocketing through me.

Okay, that one really hurt.

I can't breathe! I can't breathe!

I wrestle for air, making these weird gagging noises as I sink to my knees.

He gives me a few seconds' reprieve before snatching my arm and hauling me back to my feet.

"You promise me, Hailey! You stop spreading lies, or I'm not letting you leave."

I want to argue back that I wouldn't be spreading lies. He just admitted it to me before, and his behavior right now tells me he's a drug-dealing asshole. All I'd be doing is telling the truth!

I can't believe I thought he was good. He's a freaking psycho!

"Let me go." I start hitting his arm, scratching and clawing to get him off me.

He bats off my attack, squeezing my arm so hard his nails dig into my skin. His other hand fists my hair.

Jerking my head back, he glares down at me. "I'm

gonna hurt you. If you don't promise to keep your mouth shut about any of this, you'll regret it."

The wild look in his eyes tells me the truth. It also tells me that if I don't keep my promise, I'll pay a high price.

Closing my eyes, I feel helpless, which is one of the worst feelings in the world.

Tears trail down my cheeks as I softly whisper, "I promise."

"Look at me!" He gives me a hard shake.

My eyes pop open, and I stare at him. "I promise. Now take me home."

"One word." He holds up his finger. "You say one word to *anybody* and you *will* pay."

My head jerks up and down. I don't know what else to do. My body feels like limp noodles as he lets me go and shoves me toward his car. With shaking hands, I try to open the door and get inside, but he has to help me in the end. Slamming the door shut behind me, he lets out a growl as he stalks around the car. I would bolt and run home, but it's miles away, and I'm smart enough to know that arriving home hours after dark will only cause questions, questions I'm not supposed to answer.

Resting my hand on my stomach, I don't say a word as we drive back toward town.

"It didn't have to be this way," Josh keeps muttering. "We were good together. Dammit!"

He tuts and mumbles curses under his breath.

"Why!" he shouts at one point. "Why couldn't you just believe me!"

I flinch and press my body against the car door, clenching my trembling jaw and refusing to look at him.

He drops me off in my usual spot, about half a mile from home.

I grab my backpack and keep my eyes on the ground. I'm ready to sprint from the car, but Josh stops me with a quick reminder. "One word." He holds up his finger, then points it at me. "I'll be watching, and I'll know if you don't keep your promise. I will *know*."

The cold chill that races over my skin makes my legs buckle. As soon as he drives away, I slump onto the ground, crawling back to rest against the big old oak tree and pulling my knees to my chest.

I let the pain run through me, my stomach aching as fear gnaws on my insides.

How I'm going to pretend that everything is fine after this, I'm not sure. I guess I'll just have to keep my head down and try to avoid people as much as possible. At least until this aching terror subsides and I feel strong enough to play the most important game of pretend that I ever have.

17

TRUTH ON A TREE STUMP

Jackson

I CHECKED in with Michael and asked if I could skip out on chores. At first I didn't think he was going to let me, so I had to tell him it was about Hailey.

I didn't mention Josh at all, just that we'd had a fight and I didn't think I could concentrate on anything until I'd smoothed things over with her.

"I get that, man." He raised his eyebrows, knowing the feeling all too well. Not that he and Annie fight much, but when Annie gets hopping mad, it's like facing an erupting volcano, and Michael will do anything to make up with her as fast as possible.

Checking my watch, I cruise into town knowing I've

got nearly an hour and a half before I have to be back for Arley's picnic. I also want time to buy a few cupcakes before returning home. Calculating the math, I figure I've got just under an hour with Hailey, which will hopefully be enough time to say my apology and beg her to forgive me.

Man, I hope she forgives me.

I still don't know exactly what I'm gonna say to her. My speech has changed a hundred times since I started working on it in bed last night. I have multiple openings, and I'm not sure which one to use.

They're all genuine, but do I really want to apologize for having her back?

Definitely not.

I shouldn't have stalked her boyfriend, I guess. I can definitely apologize for that. But it's hard. I'm kind of feeling justified in wanting to protect her, but pushing her away and pissing her off isn't the answer.

How do I make my apology genuine when I don't regret what I did?

I kinda yelled at her on the way to school. Maybe I should apologize for that first.

As I pull up outside her house, I drum my fingers on the steering wheel and steal a couple of moments to settle my thumping heart.

It doesn't work.

My heart is freaking pounding as I make my way up the path and take the stairs to her front door two at a time.

Three quick raps on the wood and I step back to wait.

Hailey's mom opens the door and greets me with a warm smile. "Hi, Jackson. How're you doing this morning?"

"Good, thanks. Is Hailey home?"

"I'm sorry. She's not here right now. I haven't even seen her this morning, but she left a note saying she went for a run and wouldn't be home for a couple hours."

Huh. So a long run, then. She must be upset.

Dammit.

"I'll check out the trail running parallel to Harris Creek. That's the long one she tends to go for."

Hailey's mom grins. "You know my girl so well."

It's an effort to smile in response. My lips feel heavy as I spin and lope back down the stairs. Deciding to take the truck, I drive to the end of the trail so I can be waiting for her when she gets there.

Her usual routine is to walk to the trailhead as a warm-up, run the trail, stop for a rest, then run home again.

I've done it with her enough times to know.

Picking up my pace, I speed to the trail's end, hoping not to miss her. I should have asked her mom what time she left.

Praying the way Aunt Nell taught me to, I mutter under my breath until I reach the dirt parking lot.

When I arrive, there are no other cars in sight, which is good, because all I can see is Hailey perched on a tree stump bawling her eyes out.

"Oh shit," I whisper, jerking to a stop and jumping out of the truck.

She hasn't heard me yet. The pods in her ears must be making her oblivious to the outside world. I take it slow, not wanting to startle her.

She's making these hiccupping sounds like you do when the sobs are deep and gut-wrenching.

I kind of want to pull her into a hug, she looks so upset, but I doubt she'll want me to do that. Her shirt's all sweaty, and although that doesn't bother me, she'll probably complain that it's gross and she doesn't want me touching her.

Plus, I kind of pissed her off yesterday. Heck, she might not even want me here. But I can't just walk away. Not until I've checked that she's okay.

"Hailey?" I step up behind her.

She spins with a gasp, bulging her eyes, then whipping back around to wipe her tears away.

"Hey." I crouch down beside her, my heart physically hurting.

Dammit! I made her cry.

I'm such a freaking jerk!

She slips the pods out of her ears and sniffs, slashing more tears off her cheeks and looking away from me.

I reach for her but don't know where to put my hand. Do I rest it on her leg? That seems too forward when she's in tiny running shorts. Do I touch her face? No, a little too intimate.

Maybe her back?

Ugh, just shut up and stop thinking so hard!

"Hailey, I'm so sorry," I blurt, resting my hand on the edge of the tree stump. "I was wrong, okay? I shouldn't have followed your boyfriend like that. I shouldn't have yelled at you and said those mean things. I'm a total jerk. And now I've made you cry."

"It's not you," she mumbles, then flinches, quickly looking at me and correcting herself. "Okay, it's a little bit you."

My shoulders slump and I carefully touch her face, wiping her tears with my thumb. She looks so vulnerable I can hardly stand it.

"I'm sorry," I whisper. "I'm so sorry. Please forgive me."

New tears line her lashes. "You don't have to keep apologizing." She lets out a shaky breath and then looks at me like she's trying to decide what to say.

I watch her, my eyebrows wrinkling at the mix of emotions darting across her face. Does she want to smile because I'm here, start bawling again, or...?

My stomach clenches. I swear I just saw fear in her eyes.

"What is it?" I whisper.

"You were right about Josh." She rushes out the words so fast and so soft, I nearly miss them.

I go still, not wanting to breathe as I silently repeat what she just said.

The look on her face is warning me or something. I'm not sure what this is totally about, but I feel like her omission is costing a lot.

"He deals drugs? He told you?"

Her face bunches, her hand trembling as she presses

her finger into her eye and rasps, "I shouldn't be telling you this."

"You know you can tell me anything. I'll help you. Whatever you need."

She sniffs and takes in another hiccupping breath. "I tried to talk to him about it. He denied everything, of course, but I could tell he was lying. So, I called him on it, and then he got *really* mad." Her voice pitches, her breath catching as another sob rattles her.

My eyebrows dip. An ugly foreboding brews as I rasp out the question... "How mad?"

Hailey's lips tremble, her eyes darting to my face before her voice goes so soft it's hard to hear. "He slapped me, and then he... he punched me."

"What?" Anger fires hard and fast through my system. I can't keep my voice down as I scan her body. "Where? Are you hurt?"

"It hurt at the time, but not so much anymore." Her fingers tremble over her stomach. "It was really scary. I couldn't breathe."

"I'm gonna break every one of his fingers."

"No." Hailey grabs my shirt, fisting the fabric. There's that fear again. Stark terror. It's written all over her face. "He made me promise not to tell anybody. He said if I did that he'd hurt me and I'd regret it."

"He can't say that to you." My voice is dark and deep. I've never heard it like this before.

"I don't want you to go anywhere near him. I don't want you getting hurt or mixed up in this. I just..." She shakes her head. "I just want to forget he even existed in my life."

"Hailey." I hold the sides of her face as she starts to cry again. "You know we can't do that. He deals drugs, he hit you, he threatened you. Staying silent…"

She sobs and starts to crumple. I catch her against me, resting her head on my shoulder and rubbing her back.

"I don't know what to do." She whimpers. "I mean, I do. I know what I *should* do, but I'm terrified. He said he'd be watching me."

My muscles vibrate with rage. I swear I've never felt anything like this before, but he threatened her. Scared her! Hurt her!

I want to maim that asshole.

"It's okay," I soothe. "I know you're scared, but we can go to the police, contact the sheriff. I'll help you. I'll protect you. I won't let him touch you again. I swear, I'll do whatever it takes to keep you safe."

With another soft sob, she wraps her arms around my shoulders and clings tight. Splaying my hand across her back, I pull her against me, refusing to let go. I'll hold her for as long as she needs me to. I'll be whatever she needs me to be.

And I'll be true to my word.

I *will* do everything in my power to keep her safe. I don't care what it takes.

18

THE RIGHT THING

Hailey

JACKSON'S ARMS around me help to ease the fear and the ugly sobs. As my body starts to settle, I become aware of my sweaty shirt and how gross I must smell.

But I don't want to move.

I love the way Jackson's fingers are splayed on my back, digging in just a little, like he's keeping me together. His anger over what Josh did is this weird comfort. He promised to protect me, do whatever it takes, and I actually believe him.

Because he's my best friend, and he's not a liar.

I can't believe I ever doubted him! I can't believe I stood up for stupid Josh!

I don't want Jackson getting mixed up with all this, but maybe he could help me talk to the police or the sheriff. Maybe I can break my promise to Josh and do the right thing.

It kept me up last night as I tossed and turned, trying to figure out what to do. I kept switching from staying silent to telling everyone. The nighttime creaks in the house made me flinch, and the wind under the eaves sounded like Josh breaking in to silence me for good.

In the end, fear won out, and I stared into the darkness until I thought I might lose my mind.

This morning, I had to get out of the house before Mom saw me. I had to run. I thought it'd clear my head, but it just made me cry.

And then Jackson arrived.

How could I not tell him?

He's my best friend, the one I've always relied on and trusted.

Sitting back, I rest my hands on his shoulders and gaze at him, loving the tender look in his brown eyes.

He's so gorgeous. My gaze travels over his face, then stops when I get to his mouth. I've always wanted to kiss him. I've dreamed about what it would feel like to press our mouths together, to explore that wonderment.

I swallow, my eyes darting back to Jackson's. He's seeing what I'm feeling.

His hopeful smile is so endearing.

I want him.

I've always wanted him.

"Kiss me," I whisper, leaning for his mouth.

He doesn't hesitate this time, doesn't jerk back like I just asked him to jump off the top of the Empire State Building.

My humiliation over that moment is lost as I press my lips against his and finally after all this time experience the wonders of kissing Jackson Wilson.

His lips are soft and tentative at first, but then that awkward moment passes and we get over the fact that we're finally doing this. It's like a little switch inside my brain goes, "About time!" and everything clicks into place.

Rising to his knees, he holds my face before running his hand across my shoulders and down my back, leaning into the kiss like I'm pure oxygen. Like I'm the only thing keeping him alive.

I rise to this task, tipping my head and deepening the kiss. Threading my fingers into his hair, I let go of whatever the hell has been holding me back. All this pent-up longing and pining disintegrates, and all that remains is this kiss.

Jackson.

I'm kissing Jackson.

And it's better than anything.

It's all consuming. It's monumental. I never want to stop doing this!

"Hey!" someone shouts, snatching my shirt and pulling me backward. "What the fuck do you think you're doing?" Josh shoves Jackson back. "Get your hands off my girl."

It takes all of two seconds for Jackson to recover from the surprise attack and scramble back to his feet.

"She's not your girl," he barks, looking ready to attack. I've never seen such rage on him before.

I jump up, placing myself between them. I won't let Jackson get hurt over this.

"No! You're not fighting. Josh, it's over." I glare at him. "Of course it's over! You hit me. Now get out of here." I point to his car, wishing my voice was louder, stronger, more intimidating.

Josh's eyes flash, and he snatches my arm. "Fine. You wanna get out of here? Let's go.

"Ow!" I try to wrestle free of his relentless grip, but he's too strong, and yet again my clawing fingers seem useless.

"Let her go!" Jackson comes after Josh like a freaking wild animal. With a growl, he tackles Josh around the waist, knocking him to the ground.

I'm pushed off my feet and land with a crash, my knees scraping across the dirt and loose stones on the edge of the parking lot.

Ow. Shakes course through me as my body absorbs the impact.

It hurts, it freaking hurts, but I don't have time to focus on the blood trickling down my legs. Jumping up, I spin in time to see Josh drive his fist into Jackson's face. His arm is like a piston as he straddles Jackson and pounds him senseless.

"Stop! Stop it!" I rush over, jumping on Josh's back and trying to wrench him away.

He's so much stronger than I thought he was, and I'm

grunting and struggling, desperate to save Jackson from this attack.

"Leave him alone!" I screech. "I'll go with you. Just don't touch him. I'll go."

"No." Jackson groans from the ground, rolling over to try and sit up.

His face is a mess, blood dripping from his lips and nose.

"Hailey." He reaches out for me, and I want to run to him, but Josh grabs me around the waist, lifting me off my feet and carrying me to his car.

"No! Let me go!" I kick and writhe.

"You said you'd come," Josh spits. "Shut up and get in!"

He throws me toward his car and I crash into it, banging my elbow and crying out as my nerves throw a hissy fit.

"Hailey!" Jackson staggers to his feet, swaying unsteadily.

"It's okay. Lie down. Don't get up." Clutching my elbow, I try to caution him as I slip into the car.

Josh slams the door in my face and starts yelling. "Don't try to call the police or some bullshit. I'll kill her if you do. You hear me?"

Jackson's already pale face drains to a grayish white. He looks about ready to pass out, and when Josh reverses, I whip around in my seat, trying to make sure Jackson's okay.

"Stop it," Josh snaps, pushing me around so I'm facing

out the front again. "I told you to keep your mouth shut, but you blabbed to that asshole, didn't you? Huh?"

I swallow, refusing to open my mouth.

I don't know what's coming. The only thing I do know is that Jackson is safe, and if I hadn't agreed to get in this car, I'm sure Josh would have kept punching him until he was dead.

I did the right thing.

Closing my eyes, I try to ward off the dread simmering through me.

Don't think about what's next. Just think about the fact that Jackson is alive.

19

HOT PURSUIT

I CAN BARELY SEE STRAIGHT. My head is freaking swimming as I stagger to my truck and wrestle with the handle.

Yep, driving right now is probably a stupid idea, but I'm not letting that douchebag take off with Hailey.

Panic claws at me as I start the engine and jerk the wheel. Loose stones spray out from my back tires when I punch the gas and accelerate out of the parking lot. I hit the country road and floor it, swiping the blood streaming out of my nose.

Dammit.

When I tackled the guy, I hit my head on the landing.

It totally dazed me, and I couldn't fight back quick enough. Before I knew what was happening, he was on top of me and ramming his fist into my face like I was his own personal punching bag.

My nose is numb, but my teeth feel like they've been rattled out of my gums. My cheek has its own heartbeat, and my head is spinning slightly as I race after Josh's car.

I spot it in the distance and press the gas a little harder. I've got to get to Hailey.

Spotting my phone sliding across the dash, I reach for it, fumbling the hardware and cursing as it drops into the footwell.

"Dammit," I sputter, blood spraying onto the wheel.

My lips are puffy and tender, and I must have bitten my tongue when Josh was punching me.

Keeping an eye on the road, I try to feel around the floor for my phone. If I can just call Michael or Deeks. No, Cooper. He's the most kick-ass. He basically saved that resort from those hostage takers. He can help me save Hailey.

"Come on," I whine, my fingertips brushing my phone before it slips back out of reach. "Shit!"

Gripping the wheel, I forget about Cooper and will this truck to go faster. I'm catching up. Josh's vehicle gets close enough for me to see the back of his stupid head.

Now what do I do?

I can't exactly ram it. Hailey's in the front seat, and I don't want her getting hurt.

Blasting my horn, I come right up behind Josh's car.

"Pull over!" I shout, not that he'll hear me.

Blasting the horn again, I swerve out around him, crossing into the other lane and trying to get up alongside him.

"Pull over!" I shout again, and I know he can read my lips.

His face twists into an angry scowl as he jerks the wheel and rams into me.

I wasn't expecting that, and the truck veers off to the side. I gasp, trying to get control of the wheel, but he goes and smashes into me a second time. At this speed, I'm not quick enough to control the truck. Slamming on the brakes, I jerk and start spinning, the movement throwing me sideways.

"Ahhh!" I grip the wheel, sensing my fate before it even hits.

As the truck dives headfirst into the ditch, my head smashes into something hard, and everything goes instantly black.

20

THE BEST IN ALL THE LAND

DEEKS WEAVES Arley's hair into a French braid. He's taking his time, trying to make it look as good as the YouTube clip that taught him how to do this. Kena thinks it's adorable and sexy that he braids Arley's hair. He's not sure how those two go together, but he doesn't care. If it makes Kena give him her "I want you" smile, then he'll do it until the day he dies.

But that's not the only reason. Secretly, he loves it. Arley is always so patient with him. She's sat through many hair disasters and never once judged him for it.

Right now, she's watching the movie *Annie* and humming along to "You're Never Fully Dressed Without a Smile." She's seen this movie so many freaking times, but she loves it. Even though it came out decades ago, the original is still her favorite, and she's memorized every song, begged him to dye her hair red, and even convinced Ashlyn to buy her that famous red Annie dress for Christmas. She wore it for about a week solid before they had to bribe her to take it off and wash it.

Today, Kena managed to persuade her into a pair of jeans and a checkered shirt.

"It's more appropriate for a picnic. You know, since you'll be sitting on a rug and stuff. You can cross your legs and not worry about anyone seeing your underwear."

That made Arley giggle. She's still at that age that any toilet humor or talk of underclothes is the funniest thing.

Apparently she'll outgrow it soon, but only time will tell. Kena still gets the giggles when someone farts, so there's really no knowing for sure.

"Okay, all done." Deeks twists the hair tie around the bottom of the braid and lays it over her shoulder.

Arley gently investigates his handiwork with her fingers before spinning with a hug. "Thanks, Dee Dee. You're the best hairdresser in all the land."

Deeks cracks up laughing. "All the land, huh? That's pretty awesome."

"Oh, you are!" She kisses his cheek and makes his heart melt.

He gives her a squeeze. "You're welcome, little one. Anytime."

"I'm gonna go find Jackson!" Jumping over the back of the couch, she avoids a telling off because Deeks doesn't worry about that kind of thing.

Barreling toward the stairs, she nearly takes out Kena and yells an apology over her shoulder.

Kena laughs and saunters to the couch. "Her hair looks great."

"Apparently I'm the best in all the land."

"Oh, well, I could have told you that." She wiggles her eyebrows at him.

Deeks drinks in her smile, loving the way her wet strands of hair drape over her shoulders. She always looks so sexy after taking a shower. His thoughts fly to what they could do once Arley and Jackson leave for the picnic. The magnetic pull for his lady grows with intensity, until the word *marriage* starts blasting in his brain and he sits back with a sigh.

It's been eating at him, and he knows he needs to say something, but he's just not sure how to begin a conversation like that.

Kena walks around the couch and straddles his lap. "Okay, what is up with you this week?"

Unable to help himself, he grabs her butt and gives it a little squeeze. "What do you mean?"

"The last few days you've been quiet and tense. I was letting you brood, but it's starting to annoy me now, so talk, Deeks."

He sighs and tips his head back.

"No sighing. I said *talk*."

With a little grin, he looks back at her, playing with the belt loops on her jeans and coming to terms with the fact that he can't get out of this. "It's nothing, really. I..." He swallows. "Things are changing. Annie's pregnant. Brody's married."

Kena giggles. "Can't believe they hid that one so well. I wouldn't be able to keep a secret like that from you guys."

Deeks grunts, obviously still sore.

"Oh come on, his apology was so sweet the other night. He nearly cried."

"He's an emotional guy." Deeks rolls his eyes.

Kena tips her head with a silent reprimand. "Let it go. Forgive him."

"I have. I will. It's... I was just annoyed he didn't tell us."

"And you could see from his apology that he was annoyed with himself too. They made a mistake. And it's not like it can happen again. Jake and Carmen are already engaged, and you know their wedding is going to be a San Francisco highlight. And now that Annie and Michael are engaged, there are no more surprises."

Deeks pauses, studying her face before carefully asking, "So... no surprises from us, either?"

"Huh?" Kena's confused expression has always been so cute.

Deeks fights his grin, the gravity of his question helping to wipe it off his face. "Do you want to get married?"

Her eyebrows pop up with surprise. "Oh! Uh... do you? I mean, are you legit asking me right now?"

"No. I..." He winces. "Do you want me to?"

She goes still for a moment, looking off to the side while she obviously thinks about it.

After a torturous pause that's way too long, she finally lets out a breath and looks back at him. "Um... I don't need you to. I mean, is that what this is about? You've been all mopey this week because you're worried that I'm gonna demand some kind of proposal from you? Because if that's the case, I don't think you know me well enough to be sharing my bed."

He snickers and shakes his head. "We've never talked about it." Taking a breath, he gently cups her cheeks, brushing his thumb across her lips before whispering, "I'm serious. Do you want to marry me?"

Her full lips rise into a smile. "I would if you wanted, but I don't *need* to."

His chest blooms with love so strong and fast he feels like he could float to the ceiling.

Holding his wrists, she gives them a light squeeze. "I love you, Deeks. Whether we're married or not, that doesn't change a thing for me. We're gonna be together forever, right?"

"Yeah." He nods.

"So…" She shrugs. "Let's just see how it goes. I mean, maybe when we have kids… *if* we have kids… we'll change our minds and want to, but I don't need to be your wife to know that I'll love you through sickness and health, for richer and poorer, and all that stuff. I want to love you exclusively, and I want to grow old with you. I don't need to be your missus for that to happen."

His smile is shaky, his eyes stinging with unexpected tears. Quickly pulling her toward him, he tries to hide this sudden flare of emotion with a kiss.

Kena's lips settle him enough to pull away and look at her again. "I love you so much. I love that I get to spend the rest of my life with you."

"Me too." She leans toward him, her smile pressing against his own.

Running his thumbs up her jawline, he threads his fingers into her hair and sinks into the kiss. It's a luxurious, deep feeling that has that double effect of calming and exciting him.

It's a strange contradiction, but he can't get enough of it. Wrapping his arm around her butt, he pulls her closer and is starting to imagine the afternoon ahead when thumping feet on wooden floors makes him draw back.

"What's the matter?" Kena's face bunches when she looks across the room.

Deeks glances over his shoulder and spots Arley's upset little pout. "I can't find Jackson. He's not here."

21

BATTERED & BRUISED

A BAND of pain is wrapped around my head. With a soft groan, I reach for my forehead, hoping to ease the pounding in my skull.

Wait, why are my hands tied?

I want to spring my eyes open and find out, but I'm still struggling to move.

"Jackson," someone whispers my name. The voice is urgent, trembling.

My eyes creep open and I blink a few times, trying to bring things into focus.

Gentle fingers run around my ear, smoothing my hair back, and as my vision clears, I see Hailey above me. She's pale, her eyes puffy and scared. There's a square-ish pink mark around her mouth that I'm trying to figure out.

"Oh thank God." Her face bunches, fresh tears lining her lashes. "I thought you might never wake up."

She continues to stroke my hair. It's an awkward yet rhythmic movement, like she's running on autopilot, or she needs to keep doing it to keep herself sane.

Are her hands tied too? I try to look, but it hurts to turn my neck.

My head is in her lap, and I'm pretty sure if it weren't for my headache, this would be pure bliss.

But something's wrong.

Why are my hands tied?

Why is Hailey so afraid?

And where are we?

"What happened?" I croak.

Hailey sniffs and licks a tear off the edge of her mouth. "You were in a car accident. Your truck ended up in the ditch." She pulls in a shaky breath. "I thought you were dead, and I started screaming. I wanted to call the police, but he wouldn't let me. I begged him not to leave you there, and then I started ranting about the fact that you might get found, and if you weren't dead and you remembered anything, it'd lead the police straight to him. So he turned around and pulled you out of the truck."

"Who's he?"

She glances over her shoulder, then turns back with a frightened whisper. "Josh."

"Who?"

"My *ex*-boyfriend." She's looking miserable, angry, frightened… and suddenly it starts to come back to me.

Josh. Shaved head. Mechanic. Drugs.

Asshole.

I jerk up, my head spinning and my body aching with pains I didn't even know I had. My face is tender and sore, and my limbs feel like concrete.

"Careful." Hailey steadies me, her hand supporting my shoulder as I sway and end up leaning back against her.

She lifts her tied wrists over my head and cradles me against her, brushing her lips across my cheek.

"I think you've got a concussion. You need to take it easy."

"Are you okay?" I reach for her face, skimming my fingers under her chin. "Did he hurt you?"

"No." Her voice is small. Too small. Too terrified.

Shit, I have to get her out of this place!

"But he tied us up and shoved duct tape over my mouth. As soon as he left, I ripped it off." She winces, and I know it must have hurt.

"Where are we?"

"In his basement. He threw you down here, and I ran in after you. He didn't want us together, but I screamed that you were unconscious. He slapped me for that one."

Anger flashes through me.

"And then he dragged you around the corner and tied you up, scoffing and saying you were probably in a coma anyway. That you might never wake up." Her voice quakes, and she has to suck in a shaky breath before she can continue. "Then he tied my wrists and ankles with this stupid rope. As soon as he bolted the door, I crawled over to you. I haven't looked for an escape yet. I was too worried about you. How bad are you hurting?"

I close my eyes and do a mental check. I don't want to admit how much my body aches. Nothing feels broken. I'm just battered, bruised.

"I'll be okay. I don't think anything is broken," I murmur.

Hailey rests her hand against my cheek, concern filling her pretty eyes. "I'm worried about your head."

I try for a smile, my lips curling easily as I gaze at her. "I'm gonna be fine. But we've got to get out of here."

"I know." She nods.

"Let's start with the ropes." She lifts her arms back over my head and shows me her wrists. I get to work, picking at the knots, grateful that Josh was dumb enough to bind our hands in front of us. His knots are pretty damn good though, and I have to use my teeth. I eventually manage to loosen them enough to set Hailey free. She rubs her tender wrists before getting to work on the ropes binding me.

Soon enough, we're free and ready to take a look around this dank basement.

"Help me to stand?" I ask.

"Are you sure?"

"Yeah."

Taking our time, Hailey slowly helps me to my feet. I notice the nasty grazes on her knees, but she won't let me fuss about it.

"It's just blood. I'm fine."

"It looks nasty, and sore."

"It's nothing. Honest. Here."

She places my hand against the wall, and I steady myself. The world wants to spin, but I suck in a few deep breaths, and as I find my equilibrium, my vision clears. Yeah, that's better. I'm feeling stronger already.

I can do this.

I have to.

There's no way we're rotting down here in this foul-smelling dump. All we need is to find a way out.

22

SOMETHING TEENAGER-Y

KENA DOESN'T SAY much on the way into town. She's too pissed off to really talk.

Poor, sweet Arley is sitting in the back seat, quietly sniffing as she tries not to cry over the fact that her favorite person on the entire planet bailed on her. Not only that, the jerk isn't even answering his phone, so Kena doesn't have the satisfaction of giving him an earful.

You don't stand up your date, especially if she's an adoring eight-year-old who thinks you hung the freaking moon.

When Kena eventually finds Jackson, they will be having serious words.

No. *She* will be having the words. He can just stand there, shut up, and take it!

"Nearly there, sweet girl." Kena forces a smile, trying to keep her tone light and upbeat.

To try and make Arley feel better, she's driving her into Harborton so they can go to Joyous Cupcakes for a treat.

Having spent nearly half an hour searching the property for Jackson, they gave up. Deeks said he'd stay in case Jackson returned, while Kena agreed to take a crying Arley into town.

Parking a couple stores down from the delicious cupcake shop, Kena takes Arley's hand and tries to walk with a bounce, but it's kind of hard to do. She's riled, and poor little Arley is so sad. Jackson's never let her down like this before. He really is going through a selfish teenage phase. The sleeping in, the skipping school, the lack of communication. They can't let it go on. The adults in the house need to sit down and come up with a decent action plan.

The bell dings above the door as they enter, and the sight of all those delicious treats seems to brighten Arley's mood, as does the appearance of Indy.

"Hey, you guys!" Indy beams at them from one of the little tables in the corner.

She's set up in the sun, sipping coffee and nibbling on a slice of some kind.

"Hey." Kena approaches her table. "What are you doing here?"

"Just taking a quick break. I'm supposed to be studying for a test, but my brain is swimming. Brody ordered me out of the house for a breather while he cleans the bathroom and kitchen for us."

"Oh my gosh, dream boat!"

"I know, right? Sweetest guy on the planet." She sips her coffee, then grins up at Kena. "What are you guys doing here? Out for a girls' date?"

Kena glances over her shoulder. Satisfied that Arley is engaged talking frosting with Joy, she slips into the chair opposite Indy and moans. "Jackson was supposed to take Arley out for a picnic today. You know, that cute little monthly date they do?"

Indy nods, her eyebrows puckering as she leans her elbows on the table.

"Yeah, well, he totally bailed on her. I'm so pissed off at him."

"He bailed? That doesn't sound like Jackson."

"I know. But he seems to be going through a very distracted, grumpy, self-involved stage at the moment. He missed his morning chores the other day. He's skipped out on school, gotten double detention."

"No way!" Indy gapes. "What is up?"

"I have no idea, but poor little Arley is paying the price, and I hate that. She's the sweetest kid. Watching her cry always kills me."

"I don't think Jackson would ever intentionally let Arley down." She shakes her head and looks out the window as if she might spot him on the street. "I wonder what he's up to right now?"

"It better be something freaking important. He's got some major explaining to do when he gets home."

Indy snickers. "Your mama bear face is kinda scary."

"Good." Kena whips out of her chair and goes to help Arley with her selection.

A few minutes later, they're joining Indy back at her table with two hot chocolates, a red velvet cupcake, and two chewy chocolate chip cookies.

"Oh man, I'm so glad Joy added in this little cafe section a few years ago. It's seriously the best." Kena sits back with a sigh, licking foamy milk off her lip and grinning at Arley.

She smiles back, then shoves half a cookie in her mouth.

Indy starts to giggle at the sight, while Kena fires the young girl a reprimanding look. "That was too much. You're not a pig."

"Oink, oink." Little bits of cookie spray out of Arley's mouth, and Indy's giggles get a little louder.

Kena rolls her eyes, trying not to laugh as well. This kid is incorrigible.

The bell above the shop door rings, and they all glance over to see who's walking in.

"Hey, Faith." Indy waves at Hailey's mother as she steps into her sister's store.

"Well, hello, ladies."

Arley beams, no doubt loving the fact that she's just been called a lady.

Faith walks over and starts a friendly conversation about what a gorgeous day it is and how much she's loving the weather. "Spring is absolutely my favorite season."

"Mine too," Kena agrees, picking up her mug and taking another sip of hot chocolate.

"Well, isn't this lovely. A girls' day out." She runs her hands down Arley's braid with an affectionate smile. "I remember when I used to take Hailey out for special little dates. I miss those times."

"Yeah, they grow up so fast, right?" Kena wrinkles her nose, playfully tweaking Arley's ear.

She giggles and takes another bite of cookie.

"She wasn't even home when I woke up this morning. She left a note to say she'd gone running. No more hopping into bed with Mama on a Saturday morning. I love and despise her independence." Faith looks to the ceiling, shaking her head. "But you've got to start letting them go at some point, right? It is kind of fun seeing them turning into adults. When Jackson showed up at my door this morning, spinning his keys around his finger, I swear I felt like I was talking to a college graduate. He looks so grown-up now, don't you think?"

"You saw Jackson?" Kena tips her head.

"Yeah, he popped by to see Hailey."

"Oh, really?" Kena shoots a look at Indy, who is so obviously trying not to smile.

She loses and can't help a grin. "Do you think he's finally figured out he's in love with her?"

Faith laughs. "Oh, I hope so! Those two. Honestly, they've been dancing around a relationship for years."

Joy walks up to the table, wrapping her arm around Faith's shoulders. "Hey, sis. Have you seen Hailey this morning? Her shift started thirty minutes ago. It's really unlike her to be this late."

"I think she's with Jackson." Faith blinks, then frowns. "She went for a run this morning, and he was going to find her..." Her voice trails off, her frown deepening. "Wait a minute. You don't think they're, you know, off doing something that maybe they shouldn't be, because

163

they're only sixteen and I'm not ready for my daughter to be doing that, do you?"

"Doing what?" Arley asks, her innocent expression too cute for words.

Joy lets out an awkward laugh. "Something teenager-y. Don't you worry, sweetie, I'm sure they're being very well behaved. I mean, they're not together, like a couple... are they?"

The dubious frowns fired her way have Joy whipping out her phone. "I'll call her again. Surely if we call enough times, she'll answer."

Once again, Joy has no luck. Kena tries Jackson again too, but his phone just rings until it switches to voice mail.

"No answer." Kena slips the phone back into her pocket, and they all share slightly worried glances.

What are those two up to right now?

23

FINALLY KISSING THE ONE

Hailey

WE MOVE QUIETLY AROUND the basement, looking for any kind of escape. The space is dimly lit, the only form of light coming from a couple narrow windows just out of reach.

I bang my shin twice and manage to kick something with my toe. By the time we finish our investigation, I'm frustrated and sore. The grazes on my knees burn, and the dried blood crusted on my skin is super gross.

Slumping back down on the floor, I resist the urge to cry more tears. I've done enough of that today. All I want to do is go home and have a hot shower. Get this sweat, blood, and dirt off me. I just want to feel safe. I want

Jackson to be okay. I want to get out of this horrible place without Josh knowing!

A shiver makes my spine twitch, and I tuck my legs up to my chest, hugging them against me as fear tries to take me out.

What if Josh comes back down here?

What if he tries to hurt us again?

What if he's leaving us here to rot?

We need water!

Food!

"Do you have your phone?" Jackson's question distracts me.

"Huh?"

"Your phone."

I shake my head with a miserable sigh. "No, I never take it running." I tug at my shorts—tight little hot pants with zero pockets. I don't like carrying it in my hand or wearing one of those running belts. Instead, I just have my AirPods and watch. It's always been enough in the past, but now I'm not sure I'll ever run without my phone again.

"You?" I glance at Jackson as he takes a seat beside me.

He rubs his forehead with a sigh. "It must still be in my truck. I've got vague memories of dropping it, but I'm not sure. That kind of feels like a dream, so I don't know if it's true."

Guilt swamps me and I reach for his face, rubbing my thumb across his cheek. "I'm sorry. This is all my fault."

"What? No it's not."

"I got together with Josh."

Jackson's eyes are kind as he rests his hand over mine. "You didn't know he was a total asshole."

"I should've been with you," I whisper, finally putting it out there. Finally letting him see the truth.

He goes still, his lips parting just a little and his eyes filling with… hope.

Yeah, that's hope I'm seeing. And it's the most beautiful thing.

Licking my lips, I swallow, then figure that a dirty basement will just have to do. Honesty can be shared anywhere, right?

"Last year, when you tried to shift our relationship to something more, I… I really wanted to, but I was scared. What if we didn't make it? What if something broke us up, and then I'd lose you for good? At least staying friends meant I still had you in my life, you know?"

He nods. "I get it."

"So, is that all we're destined to be?"

Gently taking my hand off his cheek, he kisses my knuckles with a smile. "Not if we choose to make it something more." His eyes take me in like I'm special, adored, and it does things to my heart. Good, warm, fuzzy things. "I really like you, Hailey. I mean, I care about you so much. When you told me you were with someone else, I felt like my heart was being ripped out of my chest. I want to be your boyfriend. I've wanted that for so long."

"I want that too."

"Really?"

I squeeze his hand, rubbing my thumb over his wrist and pulling him a little closer to me. He shuffles forward, his poor beat-up face just inches from mine as I gaze into his eyes and keep going with this big confession. "The whole time I was dating Josh, I was trying to convince myself that it was for the best and it was good. But deep down, I wanted you. And then when I couldn't go to prom with you, it made me so sad. I could tell I'd hurt you, but I'd hurt me too. We had a deal. And it wasn't just a deal for me. I've liked you since that first day you walked into Aunt Joy's shop. Then I got to know you and that *like* grew to so much more, but it just didn't seem to work out for us. Then I let fear stop me, and I've been trying not to regret that and be brave and move on, you know?"

"I'm not sure our hearts want us to do that." Jackson's practically beaming. Who needs light when his eyes are shining so bright?

This joyful, teary laugh bubbles up inside of me, and I lean toward him.

Careful of his tender lips, I peck him gently, but he deepens the kiss, cupping the back of my head and drawing me in.

"I don't want to hurt you," I whisper.

"You couldn't," he breathes, pulling me back for more.

I still play it safe, keeping my kisses gentle, in spite of the fact that I want to dive into his mouth. My body is electrified in ways it never has been before.

Because I'm finally kissing the one. My one.

The only guy I've ever truly wanted.

24

FROM FIRST TIMES TO FEAR

PUSHING OPEN THE FRONT DOOR, Indy walks into the fresh-smelling house and breathes in the lavender-scented air.

Oh, how I love my man.

Flicking the door shut with her butt, she walks around the corner and into their small living room to find Brody nestled on the couch reading a romance novel. The book looks too small and delicate in his big hands.

Cutest thing ever!

She couldn't love her gentle giant any more if she tried.

With a swooning grin, she waltzes over and lays a kiss on his cheek, running her hands down his chest and looking over his shoulder.

He gives her a small sound of satisfaction, his eyes still glued to the book. She reads with him until he gets to the end of the page; then he flips the book shut and turns to her.

"Hey, beautiful."

His smile is gorgeous, and she presses her mouth against his, letting her lips do the talking for her.

With another sound of appreciation, he deepens the kiss, then pulls her over the back of the couch. She lands with a little laugh, her body half in his lap while he keeps the kiss going.

She runs her hand around his neck, enjoying the sizzling moment until he pulls back and wriggles his eyebrows at her.

"I should clean the house more often."

She giggles. "Sending me out for coffee and a cupcake helps too."

"Noted." He winks and starts tracing patterns on her forehead. It feels so good, Indy closes her eyes. "I could just sense you needed a little me time."

"I wasn't actually alone for that long. Kena and Arley showed up, and then Faith and Joy came over to the table."

"Wow. Sounds super relaxing."

Indy's eyes pop open in time to see Brody pulling a funny face.

She grins and traces the logo on his T-shirt with her finger. "Hey, can I ask you something?"

"Sure."

"How old were you when you lost your virginity?"

He blinks. His surprise at the question is kind of cute. "Uh... senior year of high school. She was a cheerleader. I was on the football team. It happened at a party." He stops and gives her a dubious frown. "Do you really want to know this? It's incredibly cliché, and I'm not really proud of it."

She wrinkles her nose. "I don't need details. I was just curious about how old you were."

Leaning forward, he pecks her nose. "I always wish you were my first. I kind of hate that I gave it up to some chick whose name I can barely remember. Seems like such a waste."

Indy sits up with a grin, wrapping her arms around Brody's neck and telling him, "I'm grateful you were my first, but I'm also grateful you knew what you were doing, so no regrets, okay?"

"Yeah. Okay." Squeezing her around the waist, he nuzzles her neck, then pulls away and asks, "Why are we having this conversation anyway?"

"Well, Jackson and Hailey have gone off the radar, and we're all just wondering if they're, you know... doing it."

Brody frowns. "Off the radar?"

"Yeah, Kena can't reach him, and she's super pissed, because Jackson was supposed to be taking Arley out for their monthly date. In the end, she brought her into town for a cupcake to try and make up for it."

Brody's frown deepens. "He wouldn't let Arley down to go have sex. I mean, I know he's a hormonal sixteen-year-old, but come on, he's not a complete jackass."

Indy sits back, studying her husband's face and thinking it through. "You know what, you're right. Oh my gosh, you're *so* right." She shakes her head. "Kena was so busy ranting about him becoming a selfish teenager that I didn't even stop to think. I mean, I said it was unlike him, but she went on about him getting in trouble at school and missing morning chores. I just jumped on that train and didn't think to question it."

Worry courses through her as she gets off Brody's knee and runs for her handbag.

"I need to call Kena."

"You sound worried, babe."

"I am. If you're right, then where is he? What if something bad has happened to him and we're just sitting around complaining when we should be trying to help him?"

Brody goes a little pale, vaulting over the couch and snatching his own phone off the dining table. "I'll call Michael."

Indy nods, then lets out a frustrated grunt when Kena's phone goes to voice mail. "Hey, can you call me? I think we might be wrong about Jackson. Would he honestly ditch Arley just to do something with Hailey? That's so unlike him, right? I mean, yeah, he's been a bit off this week, but Brody's made me realize that..." She huffs and rubs her forehead. "I'm just starting to feel a little worried. What if Jackson isn't with Hailey? What if something's happened to him?"

She hangs up and spins to Brody, who is setting his phone down with a sigh. "Michael doesn't know anything, other than Jackson asked if he could head into town to see Hailey. Apparently they got in a fight and he wanted to smooth things over, but he had every intention of being back in time for Arley's picnic."

Biting her lip, Indy taps her nail on the back of her phone, nearly dropping it when it starts to ring.

"Hello?"

"Hey, it's Cooper. Michael just called to say you're looking for Jackson. Can you give me an update? I'm heading into town anyway and might detour to see if I can find him."

"Oh, you are so great, thank you." Indy gives him a quick rundown of her conversation with Faith and Joy.

"Okay. Can you find out where Hailey normally runs? I'll swing past there on my way into town."

"Yep. I'll call you back in just a sec."

With Brody's help, Indy tracks down Faith's number, and she's soon calling Cooper back with the details. Being proactive is making her feel better, so once she wraps up the call with Cooper, she snatches the car keys out of her bag.

"Do you mind if we drive around town for a bit? Maybe we could head out to the high school and check there too."

"Of course." Brody pulls her against him, kissing the top of her head. "It's gonna be okay, babe. We'll find him."

Indy nods but can't find her voice as they head outside. She's already scanning the surrounding area, her eyes alert for a sixteen-year-old boy who she loves like a nephew. A favorite nephew, a kid who won her heart the first time she met him.

25

A CHEMISTRY LAB FOR DRUG DEALERS

Jackson

AS MUCH AS I love kissing Hailey—yeah, it's even better than I imagined—we can't just stay in this stuffy pit making out. I can only ignore reality for so long. As I become aware of the hard concrete under my butt and the dull ache at the back of my skull again, I start to pull out of the kiss.

Hailey leans forward for one more, like she's addicted to my mouth. I get it. Hers is pretty freaking fine. I grin, loving the compliment and sinking into one more kiss before having to push her shoulders back.

"Oh man, I really want to keep kissing you, but we've got to get out of here, Hails."

She blinks like she's coming out of a daze, and then her skin goes pale, that fear creeping back into her eyes.

I hate it and nearly start kissing her again, just to distract her, but that won't get us anywhere. We have to get out of this place.

"I'm sorry." I hold her face. "I wish we didn't have to face this, but if we're ever going to be together the way we want to be, then we have to find a way out. We have to get to safety, alert the authorities."

"I know." She nods, her forehead wrinkling as she looks around the dimly lit space. "But we looked before and couldn't find an escape."

"Yeah." I nod. "But maybe we missed something. Come on, let's try again."

I get to my feet and am pleased that the dizzy spell only lasts for a moment. Hailey stands up beside me, resting her hand on my lower back. "Are you okay? How's your head?"

"I'm all right." I give her a closed-mouth smile and head over to the narrow windows.

They're too high to reach, but maybe if I held Hailey up?

"You thinking of lifting me up there?" she asks.

"Yeah, do you think you could squeeze through?"

"We'd probably have to smash the glass. I'm worried about the noise."

"True." My shoulders slump. "What are we gonna do?"

"Let's have another look at the lock on the door."

We head back to the rickety staircase leading up to the

bolted door. It's locked from the outside, so there's really no way we can shift the thing.

I shove my shoulder into it, giving it a good push, but all it does is rattle the bolt and not open.

"Sorry, dumb idea," Hailey murmurs.

"No, it was worth another try." I give her a kind smile, which she probably can't see in this dark patch of the basement. "Look, I know the window might make some noise, but what if Josh isn't even here? It might be worth the risk."

Hailey chews her lip. "Yeah, I guess."

"Come on. It's scary, but we have to try." Taking her hand, I lead her back to the window, scanning the shelves against the wall for something she can wrap around her hand or elbow.

I saw it in a movie once. The character wrapped a towel around their arm and then smashed the glass with their elbow. I wonder if Hailey can do it. I'm smart enough to know movie effects, and that stuff they make, that looks like glass, shatters really easily. The glass in this place might not do that, and I don't want her to get hurt.

"Do you want to lift me up so I can at least see what the window's like?" she says.

"Yeah, sure." We walk to the concrete wall and I crouch, lacing my fingers together so she can stand on my hands.

Grabbing her sneaker, I hoist her up, and she holds the edge. "Oh wait. We don't have to smash anything. Let me just... loosen... this." She grunts. The sound of old metal scraping against one another makes a loud squeak, and we both freeze. My heart is pounding as I wait for the basement doors to smash open, but nothing happens.

Hailey gets back to work, and my arms are trembling by the time she finally loosens the lock and pushes the window open.

"Can you fit through?" I grunt, hoisting her a little higher.

"Yes." She starts scrambling up the wall. "But wait, what about you?"

"Just go get help. I'll be fine."

"But I don't want to leave you." Her voice quakes.

"Hails. You can do this. You gotta go."

With a reluctant huff, she scrambles out the window. I lean against the wall, dread filling me to the brim as I close my eyes and start praying.

Please let Hailey get safely away.

Please let her find help.

Please get us out of this.

Sliding down the concrete, I rest my head back and try not to panic.

I have no idea how long I've been in the basement, but Josh didn't come to check on us once in that time, so there's a chance we've been thrown down here to deal with later.

If Hailey can sneak away undetected, then I have nothing to worry about.

A sound from the stairs makes me flinch. My eyes pop open, my nostrils flaring as my heart starts to pound.

Shit! He's coming to check on us. I can't hide the fact that Hailey's gone. He'll chase after her.

I have to try and delay him somehow.

My eyes dart across the shelves, looking for anything I can use as a weapon. Maybe I could knock Josh out and bolt up the stairs. Whatever it takes to keep Hailey safe.

I—

"Jackson!" A sharp whisper fires down the stairs, and I lean forward in time to see Hailey's legs appear. "Come on, let's go."

She waves her hand, telling me to hurry up, and I scramble to my feet, stumbling a few steps before righting myself.

"How did you—"

"No one was around, so I snuck back in to get you out. Let's hurry though, okay?"

Snatching my hand, she hauls me up the stairs, and we bolt through the door.

"Wait." I pull Hailey to a stop before she can run for freedom and take the time to relock the basement door. If anyone returns, they'll take a quick glance and assume we're still down there.

"Good idea," Hailey murmurs before pulling me along.

We run down a short hallway and—

"What's that?" I point to a sheet of plastic covering the doorway to our right.

"I don't know." Hailey's eyes dart to mine. "Please don't say you want to check it out."

"I know it's probably dumb, but..." I head toward it, lifting the sheet of plastic away and seeing what I suspected might be there.

A chemistry lab for drug dealers.

"But what?" Hailey steps up behind me, obviously frustrated, but then she lets out a gasp as she looks over my shoulder.

The small kitchen is decked out with glass bottles and beakers that line the tables, along with these weird tube-looking things filled with red liquid.

"What is this place?"

"I think it might be a meth lab," I mutter. "Guess we've got something really good to tell the police now, huh?"

"Oh, you mean better than kidnapping?"

"This is hard evidence. Kidnapping is just our word against his." I pat my pockets, momentarily forgetting I don't have my phone. "Crap. I want to take pictures."

"No, let's just go. On the way out, we'll memorize everything we can about the surrounding area so we can let the police know."

"What did you see on the way in?"

"Nothing. He threw you in the trunk of his car and then shoved me in there after you."

"What?" I can't hide my disgust.

He threw Hailey in the trunk of his car. Oh man, I want to beat Josh so bad right now. I wish I could. But that wouldn't be helping Hailey.

"Let's get out of here." Taking her hand, I'm about to find the nearest doorway when the sound of voices approaching makes us freeze.

"Oh no." Hailey sucks the words in, her breaths turning instantly punchy.

Tugging her arm, I lead her through the closest doorway, and we scramble to find a hiding place in the bedroom. It's a dirty, cramped space that stinks of cigarette smoke.

"Under here. Under here," I whisper, pulling her toward the bed.

Hailey's nose wrinkles and she swallows convulsively, but the voices are getting closer.

Ignoring the smell, we crawl under.

"Watch your knees," I whisper, worried she might open the wounds again.

I hang back, giving her time to crawl under the bed and to make sure she's completely hidden before following her.

It's a tight squeeze, the bed frame pressing my chest into the floor.

"Are you okay?" I breathe the words so softly I'm not sure she even heard me. But she nods, biting her lips together and looking anything but fine.

Threading my fingers between Hailey's, I squeeze tight and start praying again.

Please don't let him find us.

26

A BROKEN VIEW OF THE HORIZON

COOPER STEERS his truck away from the end of the running trail, trying to ward off any sense of foreboding. But he can't help it. He's not the world's best tracker, but Grandpa Ray taught him a little, and the ground near the parking lot was scuffed up pretty good.

If he were a detective, he would have said a fight probably broke out, and that's what's eating at him.

What if Jackson's got himself caught up in something?

Where's Hailey?

Stopping at the exit to the parking lot, he signals right, but before he accelerates onto the country road, he makes a last-minute decision to turn left. He's not sure what's compelling him that way. It's the opposite direction to town, but he follows his gut.

He feels a little stupid for doing it. He doesn't want to worry like Ashlyn and Annie are. They're kind of panicky, and that won't achieve anything. Jackson's sixteen. Kids that age get caught up in the moment. It's not totally implausible that he forgot about Arley, especially if Hailey's involved.

Everyone's probably just getting anxious over nothing. They'll find these two, whatever state they're in. A lecture or three later and all will be right with the world again.

He tries to keep telling himself this as he picks up speed and cruises the isolated stretch of road. Green, cattle-dotted fields spread out around him, and Cooper starts to grin. It's a view he'll never get tired of. The mountains frame the stunning landscape, and his eyes skim the horizon, his smile disintegrating when he notices a truck parked awkwardly off the side of the road.

No. Not parked. Crashed.

Sucking in a breath, Cooper accelerates forward, then slams on the brakes, pulling up behind the truck. A sick dread wells inside him as he jumps out the driver's door.

He knows this truck.

It's the secondhand one they bought for Jackson when he passed his driving test.

"No, no, no." Cooper runs around the vehicle, bile swirling in his stomach when he notices the open door with blood smeared across the handle and steering wheel.

The airbag has exploded and deflated, blood coating the nylon fabric.

"Jackson!" Cooper hollers, looking around him and spinning in a slow circle. "Jackson!"

Where the hell is he?

Running down the side of the road, Cooper searches the area, calling Jackson's name and coming up empty-handed.

He takes his time and does a thorough search of both sides of the road before admitting defeat.

The kid's not here.

"So where is he?"

Going back to the crashed vehicle, he leans in and searches the interior, but all he finds is Jackson's phone wedged behind the accelerator. The screen is cracked, and the phone's not even turning on.

Panic is trying to claw up his throat. The warning bells in his head are frickin' screaming. On shaking limbs, he walks back to his truck and lays the broken phone on the hood.

Closing his eyes, he pinches the bridge of his nose, then shoots out a breath and grabs his own phone. He wants to dial Ashlyn, but instead calls Michael. He needs to hear this first.

Clenching his jaw, he waits for two rings, and then his brother's voice is in his ear.

"Hey, Coop. You're on speaker."

Biting his lips together, he kicks the toe of his boot on the ground and softly murmurs, "Maybe it'd be better to take me off speaker."

"Don't you dare, Cooper Barrett!" Annie's southern bark is loud and fierce. "Jackson is my brother, and whatever you have to say, you say to everyone!"

Her voice is trembling, and he knows his news is only going to make her cry.

Cooper breathes in through his nose, trying to figure out the kindest way to do this.

"Hey, baby. It's me." Ashlyn's voice is a sweet caress,

and it kills him that he's probably going to make her cry too. "Did you find him?"

"I found his truck."

"Where?" Michael asks softly.

"In a ditch about five miles out of town. I don't even know the name of the road, but it's the one that heads east toward—"

"I've got a map up," Kena's voice chimes in. "I'm tracking your cell phone. I can see exactly where you are."

Cooper frowns, pulling the phone away from his face to check the screen, then looking up at the sky. "You can track my phone?"

"Of course I can. I would have done it sooner, but I've only just gotten home. My laptop is now up and running. I can see Jackson's phone too. Right next to you."

"Yeah, I've got it here, but it's smashed up."

"Why?" Annie snaps. "Why's it broken?"

"Annie, I'm really sorry, but Jackson's truck is in a ditch. He's been in some kind of accident."

There's a sharp gasp and then her voice is trembling. "Is he all right?"

"I don't know. He's not here."

"What? But—"

"Yeah, it's weird," Cooper interrupts, hearing the tears in her voice and wanting to cut them off. "Something is definitely wrong about this whole thing."

"Can you see any other tire tracks around the vehicle?" Ashlyn asks.

Cooper scans the ground nearby. "Nothing obvious."

"He might have been found by someone already. An

ambulance might be taking him to the hospital right now."

"Then why haven't they contacted us?" Michael tuts while Cooper pictures him running his hand through his hair.

"Maybe we should start calling nearby hospitals and medical centers just in case," Cooper says. "I'm gonna keep heading down this road to see what I can find."

"We're on it," Kena's voice pipes up, all business. "We'll get a phone tree going to see what we can track down. Everyone, grab your devices. Ashlyn, I want you contacting Jackson's friends."

"I don't know all of his friends."

"I know some names." Annie's voice is small and tight. It's weird for everyone to hear her like that.

"It's gonna be okay," Michael says. "We'll find him."

"Okay, Ashlyn and Annie, you get to work on that. Michael, start calling hospitals. I'll contact Jake and Carmen, see if they can't help us with some phone calls too."

"What about Deeks, Indy, and Brody?" Cooper asks.

"Deeks is distracting Arley. Indy and Brody are driving 'round town looking for him."

"Okay, I'll contact them first and give them an update." Cooper nods, feeling better now that they've got some kind of plan to go on. "Let's get to work and bring our boy home."

27

THUNDERING FOOTSTEPS

Hailey

MY ENTIRE BODY is shaking as I wrestle for oxygen in this tiny, squished-up hiding place. Trying to keep my knees off the rough carpet is impossible, and I'm pretty sure all manner of disgusting is getting embedded in my blood right now.

I try to ward off that thought, but there's nothing pleasant to distract me right now. Terror keeps seizing my heart, making it stop for a moment before kicking back into a thrumming heartbeat that makes me nauseous.

"We need to get out of here." I whisper the words so quietly I can barely hear them.

Jackson shakes his head. "Too noisy."

Closing my eyes, I resist the sobs shaking my belly. This is such a freaking nightmare!

Footsteps draw closer and I suck in a breath, holding it while my heart pounds through every part of my body.

"I can't believe you brought them back here!" It's a voice I don't recognize, older, deeper, scarier. "What the hell is wrong with you?"

"I didn't know what else to do." Josh says.

Ugh, the sound of his voice makes my skin crawl. Weird how that changeup can happen so quickly. I was kissing him only yesterday.

Puke!

Gross!

His tongue was in my mouth. I let him touch me, hold me.

I need the world's longest, hottest shower, yet that still won't be enough to cleanse me. Closing my eyes, I let the regret travel through me, slow and painful.

I wish I could take it back, and I hate that I can't.

"She was screaming in my ear about the guy and getting hysterical. Then she started going on about how he might get found and then blab about me to the police. I had to shut her up somehow, and I had to get rid of him."

"So you dragged him out of the car and locked them up in the basement? You're an idiot! These people have families who will probably be looking for them."

A grunt of disgust, and then Josh is speaking again. "He saw me, okay?"

"Saw you? What do you mean?"

"He followed me and I didn't know, and he saw me making a sale."

"Are you fucking kidding me?"

There's a sharp slap, and I flinch. That sounded like a fist on a face.

Jackson squeezes my hand, rubbing his thumb over my knuckles. He's shaking now too.

"Does she know too? Huh? Does she!"

After a dread-filled pause, Josh speaks again, a little more quietly. "She figured it out."

"Shit! I told you not to get involved with her! Didn't I say that? You were at that party to entice a few people, get us some more clients, but no, you had to go all goo-goo eyes over some sixteen-year-old. What the hell is the matter with you?"

Josh doesn't respond, and I wonder what he's thinking.

Did he seriously have goo-goo eyes for me?

After him treating me so badly yesterday, I have to question that. What was I to him? Were any of his feelings genuine? It definitely felt like they were, but then that switch-up was so sudden, so fierce.

Talk about confusing.

"If you weren't my brother, I swear I would beat you dead, you understand me?"

"Look, I'm sorry I messed up. She got the better of me. She was sweet and pretty and… I don't know, man." He huffs. "It was just nice to be around something that good, you know? I felt like I could be—"

"Stop talking shit, you sappy moron!"

Another punching sound. I wince at the pitiful grunt that follows.

"Okay, fine! You're right!" Josh shouts. "I should have known better. All bitches are the same! But I'm trying to fix this, aren't I?"

"How? By hiding them in our basement? This is insane!"

"Well, they're in there now, and I can't take it back. So we'll just have to keep them locked up until we can figure out what to do!"

Another string of swear words crescendos into the air before a sharp crash, like something's been thrown or smashed into a wall.

Everything goes quiet.

I swallow and blink. My eyes are burning, my body still trembling. I don't know how we're going to get out of this.

"Maybe they could just starve down there." The older man starts talking again.

"I did manage to pound the guy a little. Plus the car accident knocked him out. He looked kind of messed up when I threw him into the basement. Maybe he's already dead."

"What about the girl?"

"I tied her up, put duct tape on her mouth. She's probably down there crying or something. I don't know, man. But... but please don't make me kill her. I don't think I can do it."

"Argh!" The man growls. "You weak piece of shit!" A

crashing of glass makes both Jackson and me jump. I whack my head on the base of the bed and wince.

"We can't let her go," Josh's brother says. "Let's just leave 'em down there for now while we figure out a plan. Shit! If they get found, we're screwed."

"Do we need to start moving the lab?" Josh asks.

"Maybe." His brother starts swearing again. "You're a pain in my ass!"

Thundering footsteps move away, and then a door slams so loudly it feels like the entire house vibrates.

We stay put, not daring to move. Jackson's still holding my hand, and I'm getting major pins and needles in my arm, but I don't want to risk moving.

"How long do we stay?" I whisper against Jackson's ear.

"I don't know."

"Do you think they've gone?"

"It's pretty quiet." Jackson nods. "Let's try sneaking away."

"Okay." I love and hate that idea, but I'm not sure I can stand another second under this stinky bed.

We crawl out in stealth mode, trying to make as little noise as possible. We both have trouble standing. My foot's gone numb, and Jackson's still a little unsteady on his feet. We take a moment to gain our balance before sneaking to the bedroom door.

The hinges let out a soft creak when we try to open it. We both freeze, not daring to breathe as we listen to the sounds around the house.

But all seems quiet.

Jackson gives me a little nod, and I follow him out the door, squeezing through the narrow opening and creeping toward the front door I snuck in to get Jackson out.

As we approach the right-hand turn, I glance down the hallway.

My blood runs cold.

The basement door.

It's open.

"What the fu— Isaac!" Josh shouts from below. "They're gone!"

Darting for the front door, we fumble the lock open and bolt outside.

"Run. Run!" Jackson jumps off the back step and starts hauling ass across the field.

I have no idea where we're going, but I chase him blindly, hoping we don't get spotted. Hoping we can reach the main road. Hoping some car will just happen to drive by and help us.

Please, please, please!

I pump my arms and beg the universe to throw out a helping hand.

I don't want to die out here on this farm in the middle of nowhere. I don't want to get taken down by two dirty meth dealers!

Help us!

28

PHONE CALLS AND INTERNET HACKING

CARMEN'S TRYING her best not to panic as she makes yet another phone call. When she first heard from Kena, she thought it was going to be some update about Annie. Maybe the start of a wedding planning conversation or some news about her pregnancy. The last thing she wanted to hear was that Jackson is missing and all they've found is his crashed truck and a broken cell phone.

She got in touch with Hailey's mom, because that's what Kena asked her to do, and she's now working through the list of friends given to her. Hailey's mom and stepfather have joined the hunt, because Hailey hasn't returned from her run.

It's a small comfort knowing that Jackson and Hailey are most likely together, but where are they?

Hailey's friends, Simone and Petra, were no help. Their answers and tiny little voices were shifty, and Carmen couldn't help feeling like they were both covering for Hailey somehow.

"What have you been up to, Hailey Parker?" Carmen taps her pen on the table while Jake continues to stay online with Michael.

The Barretts have shifted into full-scale "Find Jackson" mode, and everyone is playing their part.

Jake clicks away on his computer while he keeps the line with Kena open.

"Hello?"

Carmen stops tapping the second the girl answers the phone. "Hi. Natasha?"

"Just Tash. Who's this?"

"My name's Carmen. I'm part of Jackson's family."

"O-kay, so why are you calling me?"

"Well, we're not sure where he is right now. He doesn't have his phone on him, but we think he might be with Hailey."

"Oh yeah?" The slight hitch in Tash's voice makes Carmen's eyes narrow. Rather than trying to dodge the truth so as not to scare her away, Carmen decides to just go for it. Her 'round-the-bush tactic didn't work on Petra or Simone, and she can feel the clock ticking.

"Look, Tash, I don't want to scare you, but we think Jackson and Hailey might in trouble. We need your help. I've tried Petra and Simone, but they wouldn't tell me anything. Were they lying to cover for Hailey? If so, please don't do the same thing. I need to find them and make sure they're safe."

After a long pause that makes Carmen think the girl's about to hang up, Tash lets out a sigh and confesses, "Hailey's been seeing someone. Jackson was kind of upset about it. I'm not sure if that's relevant, but I found Hailey crying yesterday in the bathroom, and I'm wondering if there's some kind of love triangle situation going on."

"Okay. So, who is this guy she's dating?"

"His name's Josh. He's a mechanic."

Carmen starts snapping her fingers to get Jake's attention.

He spins around and she ushers him over, holding out the phone so he can listen in.

"It's supposed to be this big secret, because he's like nineteen and Hailey doesn't want her family knowing. But I got the feeling that yesterday she was having doubts, and she and Jackson got into this big fight and she was a mess. She wouldn't talk to me about it, but…" Her voice trails off into a sigh.

It sounds like a lot of high school drama, but any lead is a good one, so Carmen jumps all over it.

"What can you tell me about the mechanic?"

"Um, not much."

"Where does he work?" Carmen scribbles down the name of the auto shop and hands it to Jake.

Jumping back to his computer, he starts a search, relaying the details to Kena.

"Thanks, Tash. This is helpful. I'll see if I can find this Josh guy. Maybe he knows what's going on."

"I hope you find something. I can try calling Hailey for you."

"We've tried. She doesn't have her phone on her, and her parents say she's missing too."

"Oh no, really?" Tash's voice pitches. "Okay, well, I'll

197

start calling my friends and see what I can find out."

"I really appreciate your help." Carmen forces a smile, then hangs up, rushing over to Jake's side. "Did you find anything?"

"Kena's hacking into the auto shop's database to try to find some information on the guy."

"Got something," Kena's voice comes through the line. "His name is Joshua DeLancey. He's new in town. Only been around a few months."

"Is there any address?" Carmen asks.

"Um… I'm looking. Phone number and oh! Here!" She starts rattling it off, and Jake looks up a map.

"That's close to where Cooper found Jackson's truck."

"I'm calling him now." Kena hangs up, and they're left with a dial tone.

Squeezing Jake's shoulder, Carmen closes her eyes and starts praying for Jackson's safety.

Please, God, let this new lead help us find Jackson. Take Cooper right to him.

Taking her hand, Jake kisses the inside of her wrist. "They'll find him."

"But what state will they find him in?"

Jake works his jaw to the side. "Brody and Indy, plus Cooper, are close to this guy's house. They're strong, capable, and damn good in a crisis. However they find Jackson, you know they'll do everything in their power to bring him home safely. It's gonna be okay."

Closing her eyes, Carmen tries to draw strength from

Jake's calm assurances. When his arms encircle her, she clings to his shoulders and presses her mouth against his shirt, determined not to give in to the foreboding panic that wants to tear her heart out.

29

WHEN THE DARKNESS CLOSES IN

MY HEAD IS SWIMMING AGAIN. I'm trying to shake off that heavy, dizzy feeling. I don't have time to pass out. We've got to get away from this place!

I try to zone in on Hailey's rapid breathing beside me.

She's pumping her arms and kind of whimpering as we run away from the house. A fence is fast approaching. We can vault that and head straight down the hill. The road must be in the distance. Hopefully when we reach that, a car or something will drive past.

Man, I feel like throwing up.

Black dots spot my vision, but I blink them out of the way when a voice starts hollering behind us!

"Get 'em!" It's a roar, like some feral animal is charging us down.

"Oh shit," Hailey puffs. "Come on. Come on."

Panic. It's the only word to describe our flailing bodies as we scramble over the fence and hit the long grass on the other side. With hidden divots twisting our ankles and the grass so thick it's like running through mud, our escape is majorly hindered.

We didn't think this through.

"Head that way!" I point to our left, spotting another fence and the gravel driveway beyond it.

Hailey darts in that direction and I follow her, sensing the rabid dogs closing in on our location. They're catching up too quickly!

"Go faster," I pant, swallowing down the hot sick in my throat.

The black dots are back.

"Ahh!" Hailey stumbles, tipping forward and landing with a hard crunch.

"Shit. Are you okay? Are you okay?" I reach for her arm, trying to help her stand, but they're on me before I can.

With the growl of a werewolf, Josh comes flying, tackling me around the waist. My shoulder hits the ground first, but I don't have time to acknowledge that pain, because Josh's fist is coming right at me again.

I manage to block the first blow and grunt, trying to roll away from him.

My head is starting to swim again, like my brain's been detached from my skull and is floating away on an iceberg.

Come on, Jackson! Stay awake!

"Let him go!" Hailey screams.

She's struggling and trying to wrestle free of the guy holding her. I don't want her to get hurt. I need to get up! Defend her!

With a snarl, I channel a little of my own wild animal and lash out, forcing Josh back before he can pound another fist in my face.

He's taken by surprise, but not for long, swinging back around with a right hook that lays me flat.

"Hey!" Someone else is shouting, but not nearby. "Get off him!"

The sound is coming closer, but the edges of my vision are being stolen by a black haze.

"Let her go!"

Deep voices.

Pounding feet.

Running closer.

I force my eyes open and see a blurry vision of Cooper launching himself at Josh. Brody's right behind him, grabbing Isaac and laying him down flat.

Hailey flops to her knees, these weird sounds coming out of her as she scrambles to my side.

"Jackson?"

My eyelids are too heavy to move. I try to lift my hand, to reach out and reassure her, but everything feels too heavy.

"No. Jackson, wake up!"

"It's okay. Hailey, let me look at him." Indy. Her voice is so calm.

"Is he gonna be okay?"

Fingers poke into my neck. "Jackson? Can you hear me? Open your eyes, buddy."

It takes every ounce of effort I have, but I manage to crack my eyes open enough to let a little sunlight in.

"I'm calling an ambulance."

Blurry colors move in front of me, but I'm wafting away again.

The world is black, with only distant voices.

"Is he okay?" Cooper asks.

"He's definitely got a concussion. I don't want to move him without a paramedic checking him over first," Indy says.

"Hey. Don't! Move!" Brody's voice.

A cry of pain.

"I'm not kidding. If you even think about touching our brother again, you'll regret it for the rest of your life."

Brother?

Is he talking about me?

"Jackson?" Hailey takes my hand, squeezing my numb digits between hers. I can't really feel her anymore.

The voices are getting quieter.

The world a little darker.

Until there's nothing.

30

ALL I WANT IS JACKSON

Hailey

EVERYONE KEEPS FUSSING, and it's driving me insane. I don't care about my grazed knees. I don't want Mom to keep sitting next to me and rubbing my hand like it's a magic lamp.

There's no genie in there, Mom!

She keeps sniffing and pressing a tissue against her nose, then asking the doctor a million unnecessary questions.

All I want to do is find Jackson and make sure he's okay. He weaved in and out of consciousness in the ambulance, and I thought I might lose my mind. Thankfully, when we got to the hospital, Indy and Brody were just behind us, so they sat with me while the doctors rushed him to the ER.

A steady stream of people showed up after that, and I have now told this story too many times to count. The police want to talk to me as well, but they're being nice enough to wait until tomorrow.

Josh and Isaac are in custody, and their house is no doubt being raided and picked apart as I talk to my brother in Portland.

"It's not fair," I whine. "All I want to do is sit by his bed for the night. Why won't she let me?"

"Because you've had a scary day, and Mom doesn't want to leave your side." Nate's talking softly, gently, like I'm a five-year-old who has just woken up from a scary dream.

Maybe I do feel a little like that, but still!

I huff. "I know that! But I'm asking for your help with an appeal here. Please!"

There's a long pause, and I think my brother's going to take Mom's side. But then he lets out a long sigh and murmurs, "You finally figured out how much you love him, huh?"

I blink. My eyes feel like they've been burning all day. They're sore and scratchy after so many tears. I rub them and lean against the hospital wall, watching Mom and Richard holding each other.

"Why did it take me so long? If I'd just listened to my heart, I wouldn't have gotten caught up with Josh."

"Don't worry, I get it. Falling for your friend can warp

your brain. It's a big risk trying to move things to the next level."

"But I knew he liked me, and I stupidly shied away."

"Because you were scared it wouldn't work out and you'd lose him for good. Seriously, I get it. Shay and I both went through the same hesitations." He starts laughing. "That's so funny. It took us getting locked in a cellar to work it out as well."

I can't help a small grin. "That *is* freaky."

"Look, pass me back to Mom. I'll see what I can do."

"Thank you. Oh my gosh, thank you. You're the best." I run over, holding out the phone to Mom. "Nate wants to talk to you."

I try to keep my expression innocent, but Aunt Joy tips her head, seeing right through it. She's always been stricter than Mom, and I'm pretty sure if she had her way, I'd be grounded for dating an older guy and sneaking around behind everyone's backs.

Yeah, so looking forward to *that* conversation. I know I'm gonna have to rehash it all in detail.

It's gonna suck.

People will be upset with me, confused by my decision. They'll be outraged by Josh's behavior and shaken by what happened to me and Jackson. I've already seen a preview of it at the hospital.

Shuffling from foot to foot, I listen to Mom's side of the conversation, my stress building when I can hear that Nate's losing.

Dammit!

"Hailey?" I spin at the sound of my name. Ashlyn's walking toward me with a glistening smile. "He's awake."

My lips part. "Awake awake? Like conscious awake?"

"Yeah." Ashlyn's smile grows. "He's asking for you."

"Oh, thank God." Tears make my belly tremble, and I chase after her, not even caring what my family thinks.

Ashlyn wraps her arm around my shoulders, helping me stop the tears before they fall.

When we reach Jackson's room, I squeeze into the crowded space. His bed is surrounded by every member of his family. It's hard to move, but people turn sideways to let me shuffle past, and I'm soon standing right next to the bed.

Bending down, I press a kiss against his cheek. "I'm so glad you're awake. How are you feeling?"

I lean back and study his face, gently skimming his cheek, careful to avoid the nasty bruise below his left eye.

"My head's still swimming a little. The doctors say I have to stay for a night or two."

"Okay."

"I've got to have another scan in the morning to check out my brain, but hopefully I'll be back at the ranch in a couple days."

The relief pulsing through me makes me want to cry.

I sniff, my stomach shuddering as I hold in the tears. I don't want to waste this time blubbering.

"Hey, can you guys give us a minute?" Jackson talks over my shoulder, and I glance back, suddenly aware of all the smiling faces beaming down at us.

It takes a little while for them all to shuffle out. Arley's protesting and crying, not wanting to leave Jack Jack while he's hurting.

"You can come back soon" Deeks is telling her. "Let's go get a drink and something to eat."

"I'm not hungry."

"I'm pretty sure hospital cafeterias have ice cream." Kena's comment makes Arley perk up.

She eyes Kena and softly asks, "What flavors?"

"Let's go find out." Deeks lifts her into his arms and carries her away.

Jackson snickers, and I spin back to face him.

His beautiful brown eyes study me, and I can see the fog has lifted from his vision. Yeah, he's gonna be okay. He's probably going to have to take it easy, and when I get home, I'll be watching every YouTube clip I possibly can about concussions and the best way to manage them.

Trailing my finger down his beat-up face, I'm overwhelmed with the big feels. Like the huge, ginormous feels. They bloom inside me, stealing my voice. All I can do is smile at him.

Jackson.

My boyfriend.

At least I hope he is.

31

FAMILY IS HOME

HAILEY'S SMILING at me like I've just offered her the world.

I grin back, lightly touching the loose locks of hair that have fallen out of her ponytail. She looks a mess.

A beautiful mess.

"Are you okay?"

"Yeah," she whispers. "I'm just glad you're okay. When you blacked out, I got really scared."

Her smile is gentle, tired. I should probably let her go home and rest, but I don't want her to leave.

Tucking the wayward locks behind her ear, I ask, "Have you spoken to the police yet?"

"Briefly, but they want to interview me tomorrow." She sighs. "I don't want to."

"I know, but it'll be okay. You didn't do anything wrong, remember?"

"I dated a—"

"You didn't know that when you started dating him." I tug her toward me, grateful she's okay, and that I was there.

The horrible thought of what Josh might have done to her will no doubt haunt me. Thank God I couldn't stand being at odds with my best friend. We've never gone more than a day or two without talking (excluding that horrible month four years ago). I hope we never go through that again. I hope we're best friends forever.

"Hey, can I ask you something?" She brushes her lips across mine before leaning back to look at me.

"Sure." I take her hand and our fingers start to dance, weaving and spinning together in a soft caress.

"Well, the truth is, I shouldn't have to ask because we made a deal, and a promise is a promise."

I laugh, immediately knowing what she's referring to. "I'd love to go to prom with you."

"Yay." Her celebration is quiet and sweet, and the look on her face is nothing but gorgeous. Man, I like her so much.

I think I love her.

I think I always have.

"Kiss me," I whisper with a smile.

She doesn't hesitate, leaning into a kiss that makes my body forget it ever got hurt in the first place.

"Okay, that's enough, you two." Brody walks into the room.

We ignore him and keep kissing until the room is nearly filled with my family again.

They start catcalling and hassling us about young love, and Hailey pulls away with an embarrassed giggle.

"We'll continue this later," I whisper.

"Hailey, your mom wants to head home. She's waiting for you." Indy gives her a kind smile to counter the news neither of us wants to hear.

Her shoulders slump, and she looks so sad.

"I'll see you tomorrow." I touch her face one last time.

"Okay." She pouts for a second, then shuffles out of the room.

No one says anything as she walks away and I close my eyes, reminding myself that she's safe and I'll see her tomorrow... if her mom will let her come visit. Aw man, I hope she doesn't get into too much trouble over the whole secret boyfriend thing.

"Has he fallen asleep?" Deeks asks.

I crack my eyes open and can't help a smile.

"Knew you were faking it." Brody clips my foot with a laugh, and I hiss. His eyes bulge with instant regret. "Crap, I didn't know you hurt your foot too. What part of your body is not sore right now?"

I can't hold in my laughter as I raise my finger and point at him.

"You're... You freaking got me." He shakes his head, biting his lips together and trying to look pissed, but I can tell he's impressed that his beat-up little brother can still share a joke.

Little brother.

His threat against Josh and Isaac is still swirling in my brain, unforgotten, even though I blacked out.

He called me his brother.

Actually, he said *our* brother.

My eyes scan their faces, all of them grinning at me like I'm important. I mean something to these people, just like they mean the world to me.

Because we're family.

We're Barretts. All of us are.

It doesn't matter who else joins the crew or where they come from. This mishmash of people has chosen to form a family, and they've made me a part of it.

The thought make my eyes glisten.

"So, got yourself a date to prom, huh?" Brody wiggles his eyebrows at me.

"What? Were you eavesdropping?"

"Totally." He shrugs, unashamed.

I throw Indy an incredulous look, but she just shakes her head. "My man, people."

Everyone laughs along with her, and I lean my head back against the pillow.

"So... is Brody right? Are you taking Hailey to the prom?" Ashlyn leans in, taking my hand and giving it a little shake.

I can't help my smug smile. "Yes I am."

"Yay!" she cheers, clapping her hands and looking at Cooper.

He grins, winking at her before looking back to me. "Nice one, man."

"Thanks."

Annie's sniffing and fussing with my pillow. "He has to get better first." Kissing my forehead, she looks down at me the way Mom used to, her watery smile filled with affection. "Don't you ever scare me like that again, you hear me?"

"I had to protect her, sis."

"I know. I just hate that you got hurt, is all." She tips her head, her blue eyes shining bright. "I'm proud of you."

"We all are." Cooper nods.

"Yeah. We love you, kid." Michael raises his chin at me. "Family wouldn't be the same without you."

"That's why we all dropped everything to come find you." Kena crosses her arms and grins at me. "We would have moved mountains for ya, buddy."

"Thanks, you guys." I swallow, emotions getting the better of me.

"Aw, c'mere." Annie wraps me in a half hug, resting her head against my shoulder and squeezing my waist.

I kiss her head and smile at my brothers and sisters.

My family.

My home.

32

A PERFECT NIGHT

Hailey

"OH MY GOSH, you look so beautiful!"

Mom and Aunt Joy are fussing again, but I don't mind so much this time.

Gazing in the mirror, I smooth my hands down my prom dress, happy with the floaty design we chose. I look like a princess. The beaded, fitted top of the dress hugs my body before soft fabric falls in waves from my waist down.

"Oh, Hailey, that color is perfect on you." Mom's gushing.

"That powder blue really makes your eyes pop." Aunt Joy kisses my cheek. "You're just stunning."

I smile, giving her a sideways hug as butterflies flutter through my system.

I'm going to the prom with Jackson. It's finally happening.

The last five weeks have been eventful with both his recovery and the fact that he's now my boyfriend. The buzz around school was insane. Small-town life means gossip spreads far and wide. By the time Jackson returned to classes, everyone knew about me getting caught up with Josh and how Jackson and I had to escape his drug house. It was kind of humiliating, and I nearly started skipping school just so I didn't have to deal with it. But Jackson showed up and we had each other's backs. Our friend group made a circle around us, and with busy classes, studying for SATs, and just life in general, things have become a blur.

But tonight is crystal clear.

Tonight, Jackson and I finally get to live out the deal we made all those years ago.

The doorbell rings and we all jump.

"Oh my gosh, he's here!" Mom hurries out of the room while Aunt Joy double-checks my hair.

"Do you want more hairspray?"

"No, it should hold." I check my reflection, making sure the long curls are still hanging the way I want them to.

"Okay, well, sweet girl, you have so much fun tonight."

"Thanks." I kiss my aunt and head downstairs, holding the banister so I don't fall in these heels I'm not used to wearing.

Jackson's in the foyer, talking to my parents. Yeah, Dad flew up for the weekend. I thought it'd be kind of awkward, but he's staying at the local bed-and-breakfast, and things have actually been really cool. He took me out for dinner last night, and we spent some time together this morning too. As always, I'll miss him when he flies back to Arizona, but I appreciate the fact that he's trying to come up more frequently.

I think my scare with Josh really rattled him.

I totter down the next few steps and pause as Jackson's head turns my way. The plastic box holding my corsage crinkles under his thumb.

He stares at me like I'm a vision, his mouth opening and closing a couple times before he manages, "You're... so amazing."

I can't help a soft giggle. "Thanks. You're pretty amazing yourself."

Walking off the bottom step, I move toward him, grinning like a goon as he places the corsage around my wrist with slightly shaking fingers.

"Aw, they're so cute," Mom whispers to her husband while Dad starts snapping photos.

"Connie's gonna want to see how beautiful you look."

I turn and smile for Dad's girlfriend; then we pose for a few more shots before finally heading out the door.

But then we have to stop on my porch.

I glance up at Jackson, my eyes slightly bulging.

"I'm sorry." He scratches the back of his neck. "They all wanted pictures. Even Carmen and Jake flew up for this." He rolls his eyes.

Laughter pops out of me as I turn back to the line of cars outside my house. It's a barrage of Barretts, all with their phones out, snapping pictures of Jackson's first prom.

"Aw. They love you." I rest my head on Jackson's shoulder, smiling until my cheeks hurt.

The Barrett clan happily takes a million pics, then tells us how beautiful we look.

Cooper, dressed in a suit and tie, escorts us to a very clean and shiny car, which he's obviously borrowed for the weekend.

"Your ride, milady." He opens the door for us, bowing low as I slip into the back seat, feeling like I'm in the middle of a fairy tale.

Waving goodbye to our two families, I snuggle back against Jackson, who rests his arm around my shoulders.

"You look really beautiful."

I tweak his suit jacket. "So do you. Handsome, I mean."

We grin at each other and share a kiss before heading out to pick up Tash and her date. By the time we get to school, we're all talking at once, excitedly speaking over one another as we leave the car.

I give Cooper a kiss on the cheek. "Thank you, chauffeur."

"Not a problem. I'll be back to pick you up later. Just text me."

"Will do. Thanks, man." Jackson waves him off, then takes me by the hand and leads me toward the decked-out school hall.

"This is it." I squeeze his fingers.

"I've been waiting for this moment for a really long time."

"Me too." Letting out a happy little squeal, we walk into our first prom together. Simone and Petra are already there, looking so beautiful, and we admire each other's outfits while we wait for the guys. Within half an hour, we're lighting up the dance floor, acting like idiots and pulling out crazy moves that have us all cracking up with laughter.

The live band spurs us on, and I'm eventually out of breath and euphoric, struggling to drink my punch as I sit on Jackson's knee and take a break on the sidelines of the dance floor.

His arm curls around my waist as he places the sweetest kiss on my cheek. "I'm having so much fun."

Placing my punch on the seat beside us, I turn to beam at him. "Me too."

I hold his chin and tug him toward me for a proper kiss. His mouth is so familiar now, yet sometimes the sensation of kissing him is so thrilling, it feels like our first one all over again. I let out a happy sigh as I sink just a little deeper into his mouth before easing back.

His smile is adoring, and I drink in his handsome face, that loved-up look in his eyes.

"I really like having you as my boyfriend, Jackson Barrett."

He grins, obviously appreciating the fact that I'm using the name he's asked me to.

Touching my cheek, he runs his fingers down to my

jawline, his smile growing even wider. "You make the world's best girlfriend, so it's working out well for both of us."

I giggle. "I seriously don't know if I could be happier. Thanks for coming to prom with me, thanks for being my best friend, and thanks for... you know... always having my back."

My expression turns serious, and he easily picks up what I'm saying.

"I'll always be there for you, Hails. No matter what happens between us, I will *always* have your back."

My lips curl into a smile, and I press it against his mouth. He cups the back of my head, sending my heart into a tailspin as he brushes his tongue across mine.

"Okay, you two." A teacher strolls past, reminding us where we are and how much PDA is appropriate.

I rest my forehead against Jackson's, and we snicker together, looking over my shoulder to watch the teacher cruising the rest of the hall.

"You know," he murmurs against my cheek. "If your kissing continues to be this sensational, I might just have to stay with you for the rest of my life."

I laugh, wrapping my arm around his neck and hugging him. "Being with my best friend forever sounds pretty good to me."

He holds me close, splaying his hand over my back and filling me with that overwhelming sense of safety and love.

Seriously. I could stay like this forever.

"Come on, you guys!" Simone runs over. "We have to dance to this one."

Snatching my wrist, she pulls me out of the hug, dragging me back onto the dance floor. Jackson jumps up, chasing after us, and we party until the clock strikes midnight.

Threading his fingers through mine, Jackson walks me back out to the parking lot. Our smiles are wide and delirious.

This has seriously been the best night ever.

"Oh, hey." Jackson pulls me to a stop just before we reach the exit.

"What?"

I laugh when he wraps his arm around my waist, lifting me off my feet and kissing me.

"Do you want to be my date to Annie and Michael's wedding?"

I blink, surprised by this question that seems to come out of nowhere.

He blushes and looks so freaking cute that I have to give him a quick kiss before responding.

"Well, that's a no-brainer." I giggle, running my fingers through his hair. "I would love to."

His smile is rich with affection. "You make me so happy."

"The feeling's mutual." I lean in, stealing one more kiss and drawing it out until a car horn starts beeping and we're forced to say goodnight to the perfect evening.

It's not so bad. Especially since I know there will be plenty more to come.

Jackson and I were always meant to be together. I can't believe it took us so long to act on that fact, but I have a feeling we won't be letting go of what we've got anytime soon.

So I say, bring on the future!

33

I'LL ALWAYS BE ONE OF THEM

THE SUN IS SHINING like it's as happy as we are.

Adjusting my tie, I smooth it down beneath my jacket and have to wonder yet again why Annie wanted suits and ties for an outdoor wedding in the scorching heat.

But I won't complain about the wet patches forming beneath my armpits or the trickles of sweat I can feel running down my back.

This is Annie's special day.

I won't complain about anything.

Clearing my throat, I scan the chairs set out in the sunlight, grinning at Hailey when she spins around to tinkle her fingers at me. She's looking hot in her little summer dress, with her hair all long and splashing over her shoulders.

Who am I kidding?

She looks hot in everything she wears.

Thank God for summer and bikinis, though. I can't wait to head down to Arizona with her in a few weeks. We've been invited to hang out with her dad and his girl-friend, plus Hailey's second brother Lucas will be there too. It should be a fun trip.

"Nearly ready." Arley's cute voice makes me spin, and I smile at her sweet self, walking down the stairs in her flower girl dress.

Kena is right behind her, holding her hand and making sure she doesn't fall and mess up the pale gold gown. It's covered with sequins at the top, then has this puffy skirt thing that seems to shimmer in the sunlight.

"Do I look pretty?" Arley looks up at me.

I crouch down so we're eye level and tell her the truth. "You are gorgeous."

She beams at me, then turns to take Kena's hand again.

"Annie's just coming out." Kena looks over her shoulder and I study her, kind of weirded out by seeing her in a silky dress with her hair done up like that.

She hates wearing fancy clothes and heels. Where are the combat boots and ripped jeans?

"You look… really gorgeous too," I murmur.

She snorts and adjusts the strap of her dress. "Thanks. I can't wait to get out of this thing. But hey, we make sacrifices for those we love, right?"

"Yeah." I chuckle when she winks at me, then turn when I hear footsteps behind me.

Annie is standing on the porch, surrounded by her bridesmaids.

All the Barrett girls are decked out in silky dresses that match the tones of Annie's stunning wedding dress.

She looks freaking amazing.

Her blond hair is piled on top of her head, with soft wisps framing her face. Then she's got this bodice thing with like gold leaf embroidered all over it before the fabric changes to this soft floaty stuff that covers her growing baby bump.

She's still really tiny, and if you didn't know, you wouldn't necessarily realize she was pregnant, but I've felt that bump. Annie made me when she swore she felt the baby move and I was the only one around.

I didn't feel anything but didn't have the heart to tell her.

She was freaking euphoric. I guess her fears over having a baby are starting to ease. It probably helps that last month, Ashlyn announced her pregnancy too.

You should have heard the screaming.

They've been like giddy schoolgirls, except every conversation they ever have now is about baby stuff.

Honestly, Arizona's gonna be a welcome break.

Annie gives me a nervous smile as the bridesmaids file past me, and I step onto the porch, offering her my arm.

"You look real pretty. Mom would be... so stoked... and proud."

"Thanks." Her blue eyes glisten.

"That mascara's waterproof, right?"

"Oh, definitely. I'm pregnant and getting married. Crying is going to be a guarantee."

"Well, try to make it down the aisle before you start blubbering, okay?" I chuckle when she lightly slaps my arm. "Hey, thanks for letting me walk you down the aisle."

She looks up at me. "Who else was I gonna ask?" Her confusion melts into a beautiful smile when she reaches up and touches my cheek. "You and me. No matter who else comes along, we've got a special bond no one can touch. Don't you go forgetting that."

"I won't."

"Okay." She goes up on tiptoes and kisses my cheek. "Now, get me to my groom before I melt in this heat."

"Try wearing a tux," I tease, helping her down the steps and making sure her dress doesn't catch on anything.

The music starts playing and Arley sets off, throwing rose petals into the grass as we begin the slow march to the natural archway Hailey and Petra spent literally hours creating. Ashlyn's friend Leo helped too. Actually, Leo helped with a lot of stuff. I seriously think he should forgo interior design for a career in wedding planning. I told his husband that at the rehearsal dinner, and he totally agreed with me.

"Here we go," I murmur to my sister, and we share a smile just before hitting the aisle.

After that, the only person Annie can see is Michael.

I nearly start laughing at the goofy, loved-up expression on his face, so I quickly avert my gaze and trail down the row of brothers.

Five Barrett boys. Actually six, once I let my sister go and move to the end of the line.

Six Barrett boys, standing right where they belong.

I know the story now. The big secret about the night Grandpa Ray died. They spared no details, and I was grateful for it.

Deeks and Cooper told me over a late night game of poker.

They even let me have a beer.

I think I needed it. The story was intense, but man, am I grateful for Grandpa Ray.

He saved these guys, and I guess he ultimately saved me too, because he left this home to his grandsons, and I was lucky enough to get pulled in for the ride.

Aunt Nell always says that Grandpa Ray is looking over us, watching as we grow up and figure out our way.

I hope I'm becoming a man he can be proud of too.

Living up to the Barrett name might not always be easy, but it will *always* be worth it.

Live justly. Love mercy. Walk humbly.

Dear Reader,

. . .

Thank you so much for reading this series. I hope you loved getting to know this family and watching each brother come home. Working with this cast of characters has been such a privilege. They will always stay with me, and I'm sure my imagination will pop back to the ranch often as I picture what this family will look like with babies and toddlers running around. I'm so happy for the future they have to look forward to.

Family is so important, and even though it's not always easy, it's always worth the fight. We've been designed to love and care for each other, to look out for one another, to always have each other's backs. That's what family does.

So, what's next for Jordan Ford?

Well, I have some pretty awesome stuffed planned. My heart wants to write more Fairy-tale Twists novels to go along with _Paper Cranes_. I have a _Beauty and the Beast_ retelling and a _Sleeping Beauty_ one I want to work on. After that, I have a series that will run like a TV show—each book a new episode involving a big cast of characters who I know you're gonna love. I don't want to give too much away, but I will definitely be sharing news as it unfolds.

· · ·

Another thing I want to do is take some time to create audiobooks for the Forever Love series. This series is set on a farm in New Zealand and follows a makeshift family as they try to navigate life after a tragic and unexpected loss. Journey with these teens as they experience the ups and downs of a new high school, first loves, broken hearts, and what it ultimately means to be friends for life.

In the meantime, while you wait for more releases, you might want to check out other books I've written that are similar to the Barrett Boys in style.

The Brotherhood Trilogy
(YA Romantic Suspense)

Ryder Bay Series
(YA Romantic Suspense)

Barlow Sisters
(YA Sports Romance/Mystery)

The Aspen Falls Novels by Melissa Pearl & Anne Cruise
(Small-town romantic suspense)

The Fugitive Novels by Melissa Pearl
(YA Contemporary Romance/Mystery)

Thank you so much for investing time in my work. I so appreciate your support and enthusiasm. If you've loved what you've read, please consider leaving a review, and if you ever want to email me to chat books, I would love to hear from you: jordan@jordanfordbooks.com.

And for a free introduction to Jordan Ford's Ryder Bay series, sign up for her newsletter here. You'll also be eligible for exclusive content, giveaways and sales.

And just before I go, I have to take a moment to thank all the people who have helped me bring this Barrett Boys series to life:

Niki, Rachael, Beth, Kelé, Karen and Kristin. Thank you for your talent, your feedback, your time and attention. You truly are the best people to work with.

My review team - thank you for loving the Barrett Boys so much and spurring me on. Your enthusiasm is the best kind of motivation.

· · ·

Thank you to my amazing Forever Love Crew. You are such a blessing to me.

Thank you to my readers. I couldn't do this job without you. Thanks for buying my books and helping me keep this dream alive.

Thank you to my amazing family. I am blessed beyond measure to be surrounded by people I love, and who fill my heart to overflowing.

And, as always, a big thank you to my creator. Thank you for all you have gifted to me. I never want to take for granted your abundant love and this life, filled with so many things to be grateful for. I love you.

xx Jordan

DEAR READER...

Thank you so much for reading this series. I hope you loved getting to know this family and watching each brother come home. Working with this cast of characters has been such a privilege. They will always stay with me, and I'm sure my imagination will pop back to the ranch often as I picture what this family will look like with babies and toddlers running around. I'm so happy for the future they have to look forward to.

Family is so important, and even though it's not always easy, it's always worth the fight. We've been designed to love and care for each other, to look out for one another, to always have each other's backs. That's what family does.

So, what's next for Jordan Ford?

Well, I have some pretty awesome stuffed planned. My heart wants to write more Fairy-tale Twists novels to go along with _Paper Cranes_. I have a _Beauty and the Beast_ retelling that I'm hoping to release soon.

In the meantime, you might want to check out other books I've written that are similar to the Barrett Boys in style…

The Brotherhood Trilogy
(_YA Romantic Suspense_)

Ryder Bay Series
(_YA Romantic Suspense_)

Barlow Sisters
(_YA Sports Romance/Mystery_)

The Aspen Falls Novels by Melissa Pearl & Anne Cruise
(_Small-town romantic suspense_)

The Fugitive Novels by Melissa Pearl
(_YA Contemporary Romance/Mystery_)

Thank you so much for investing time in my work. I so appreciate your support and enthusiasm. If you've loved what you've read, please consider leaving a review, and if you ever want to email me to chat books, I would love to hear from you: jordan@jordanfordbooks.com.

And for a free introduction to Jordan Ford's Ryder Bay series, sign up for her newsletter here. You'll also be eligible for exclusive content, giveaways and sales.

And just before I go, I have to take a moment to thank all the people who have helped me bring this Barrett Boys series to life:

Niki, Rachael, Beth, Kelé, Karen and Kristin. Thank you for your talent, your feedback, your time and attention. You truly are the best people to work with.

My review team - thank you for loving the Barrett Boys so much and spurring me on. Your enthusiasm is the best kind of motivation.

Thank you to my amazing Forever Love Crew. You are such a blessing to me.

Thank you to my readers. I couldn't do this job without you. Thanks for buying my books and helping me keep this dream alive.

Thank you to my amazing family. I am blessed beyond measure to be surrounded by people I love, and who fill my heart to overflowing.

And, as always, a big thank you to my creator. Thank you for all you have gifted to me. I never want to take for granted your abundant love and this life, filled with so many things to be grateful for. I love you.

xx Jordan

LOVE146

A way to give back...

I am passionate about telling stories of healthy love.
Unfortunately, there are some very distorted messages of
what love is out in the world today, and through my
books, I want to share the message of what real, good,
healthy love should look like.

A way for me to show this in action is by sharing my
profits with an organization that lives love on a daily
basis. Their mission is to eradicate child trafficking and
slavery from the world. They are truly an awesome
organization, and I thank you for helping me support
them.

www.love146.org

MELISSA PEARL
the ultimate romantic adventure

Melissa Pearl is a romance author writing in a variety of genres from teen paranormal romance to small-town romantic suspense. She's passionate about telling adventure-filled love stories with relatable characters who will take you on a journey.

If you're after an escape from reality, then check out her **WEBSITE**.

www.melissapearlauthor.com

Melody Sweet is the master of character journeys as she dives into the nuances of love and how it can break, heal, restore, entertain and enrich our lives. If you enjoy stories that take you on an emotional journey, then you'll love her sweet contemporary romances and romcoms.

Sophia Quinn is the pen-name of writing buddies Maggie Dallen and Melissa Pearl Guyan. Between them, they have been writing romance for 10 years and have published over 200 novels. If you like books set in small towns with big feels and romance that will capture your heart, then her books are just for you.